SNOW ON THE RANGE

A RED HART RANCH CHRISTMAS SPECIAL

SOFIA AVES

Copyright © Sofia Aves 2020

First Edition

Published by Little Quail Press

Cover Art by JS Designs Cover Art

Editing Services provided by A. Strom - Edits with a Coffee Addict

www.redpensandcoffeebeans.wordpress.com/

www.facebook.com/redpensandcoffeebeans/

ISBN 978-1-922448-11-8

CONTENTS

Brit, thank you for showing me the beauty of Montana, and convincing me to write it. Ashley, thank you for the snow.

PROLOGUE

You think you got away from me. You think you escaped unnoticed.

Blood stains my hands that should be on yours. The stench of death follows me across every border, but I will not stop until I find you.

You stole from me, from my family. Years were stolen from a man taken by violence before his time.

You will be hunted. You will be found. And you will be judged.

I will not let Sam Bernie's death be in vain.

CHAPTER I

The ranch smelled like Christmas. The fresh, woodsy scent that reminded me of the forest before the first snow covered it. Every year, the tall pines populating the mountains around us were blanketed in a heavy white coat for the winter. An undercurrent of citrus mingled with ginger spice and smoke from hearth cemented the impression in my mind.

Viola, instant Christmas.

The mountains surrounding our northern borders were already capped in white, though we hadn't had snowfall on the flats yet. Our trademark red deer grazed outside the broad windows at the front of the main house, garlands the hands had draped over the timber-framed ranch entrance a contrast to the bright sky high above. The cold already setting in, Red Hart Ranch glowed with the coming festive season.

I loved this time of year.

Grabbing an armful of foliage I'd spent hours the night before twisting sprigs of holly into, I flung the end of a garland over the curtain rail, but it didn't catch. I flung it up again and missed my mark by mere centimeters. My lip curled as I bared teeth at my nemesis. The banister had been so much easier.

I didn't usually go to quite as much effort, but I wanted greenery inside as well as out this year, for no other reason than I just wanted to make the ranch look festive. Especially with many of the hands vacating for the season before the weather closed in, and they were stuck miles from their own families at Christmas. With Dad laid up in bed, I struggled a little on my own, but it was all the more reason to bring a little laughter into the house.

This year, we could all use it.

Frustrated, I flung the garland again with a little growl as wire scratched my fingers. I cursed myself as lazy for not tying them off properly the night before, but I'd been exhausted — and slightly inebriated — by the time I'd finished my labor in the colder hours of the early morning.

I'd taken the remainder of the night's mulled wine up with me and awoken to find the pitcher empty when my eyelids had cracked open a few scant hours of heavy sleep. The meadowlark outside my window had decided to serenade his paramour, and from the way he'd attacked my window, apparently, that was me.

My body clock couldn't be reset by a late night anymore. A dawn riser never changed, or so it seemed.

I gripped the end of the garland tight, swinging it a little to build momentum, and gave it a hefty toss. A large hand caught it, flicking it neatly into position.

"You want me to do the rest?" Travis laughed at me.

"Just because you got all the tall genes," I grumbled at my twin, passing bunches of greenery over my shoulder to him. "Careful with the holly. That took me hours, and it's vicious on the fingers. I'll do the railings outside?" I held up a hand. Red puncture marks decorated most of my fingertips.

"Sounds like a good deal."

In the end, Trav helped me with the top railings too. He fussed more than I would have bothered with the finer details while I excused myself to find some painkillers. By the time I made it back downstairs, Mom had coerced my brother into the kitchen. With her hands on her hips and a stern face, she appeared to be reading him his rights. I wandered into the room to find out what he'd done to be in strife.

She spotted me as I reached for my full travel mug of coffee. The freshly roasted beans melded with the pine needles in a heady medley, though there were two more weeks until Christmas. My stomach rumbled as freshly made gingerbread wafted beneath my nose. Hunting across the countertop already laden with food prep for the holidays, I spotted the biscuit tin. Mom batted my hand away before I could snitch a treat.

"Are you two alright to get everything, then? You'll need both trucks to get supplies and to collect supplements from the vet." The vet was Rachel, and I knew who would be making that visit. I grinned inwardly as Mom pressed a list into my hand — *not Trav's* — the brilliant blue sapphire that had been passed through the family for years flashing on her finger, and shooed us out the door with a wave.

"Right. Got the list, my phone — call me when you get stuck this time, okay? And I need..." I patted my pockets then held out a hand, "my keys, please."

"You don't need that big truck to yourself, Eve. That's just plain greedy." Travis waved my keys in my face, laughing as they jingled before my narrowed eyes. He paced quickly backward to my white F350, Red Hart Ranch's logo displayed proudly on its side. A hart — a deer in its maturity — its antlers curving to form a red heart on a white background, with the letters RHR typeset into them.

My truck with the logo *I'd* designed, all those hours of learning to use photoshop under *my* belt.

"Uh-uh," I jogged after him as he turned, sprinting to the cab. I got there just as he slid the key into the ignition.

"See you in town," he called from the driver's window, the all-terrain tires kicking up dirt as he took off too fast down the long drive that led back to the road.

I watched my truck disappear into the pines that lined the driveway, muttering dark and unladylike curses under my breath as I headed for Trav's beat-up Dodge. He'd been fixing the thing for years, and I knew he'd put too many hours and too much love into it to sell — or worse, turn it into a farm truck for the hands to bash about.

Sliding into the driver's seat, I noted his keys still in the ignition. After all, I mused, why would anyone bother to steal the rust bucket, especially all the way out here? No, even in town, this wouldn't be a vehicle you'd steal.

I fervently hoped it would make it to town and back. I revved the engine hard, and the contraption started with a splutter. Cole Swindell's voice filled the cab. I grinned as I followed my brother into White Cap.

At least he had decent taste in music.

A clear ninety minutes later, I pulled up outside *Beanie's*. White Cap was named for the mountain that sat behind the township, a mirror of Red Hart, but a hundred miles of winding road and ridgelines to the south.

Smiling at the sign hanging above my friend's shop, I weaved my way between people huddling in their thick coats, clutching their shopping. The wind had a bitter edge, its icy tendrils creeping inside my coat without an invitation. I wrapped my arms around myself as I headed along the pavement. I noticed it more every time I came into town, lucky not to have the gusts so regularly at the big house. We were protected on one side by the mountain that framed Red Hart. The pasture beyond, however, took a thrashing whenever wind roared across it.

Cars and trucks cluttered Main Street. And for a town with only a few thousand occupants, that meant nearly everyone had come in, either to fulfill their shopping and gift needs or preparing for the oncoming weather. With Christmas coming along faster than any of us would have liked and the threat of a potential snowsquall on the horizon, everyone was taking the opportunity to stock up.

And that included us, too.

I extracted the list Mom had given me, craning my neck for my truck, though it would have stuck out if my brother had parked it on the main street. I grinned, turning back to the list; if Travis wasn't doing the chores Mom had set him, then he'd likely already be at the vet's seeing a certain blonde animal doctor.

The steady hum of the busy main street had nothing on the interior cacophony inside Beanie's. I looked at the sign, remembering the brief moment of horror I'd had when the original signwriter had presented the shopfront to Suzy and me years ago. The *A* where an *R* was meant to be.

I'd gaped, but in a fashion true to herself, Suzy Bernie had laughed, startling half the street on a Monday morning. She'd proclaimed the shop would forever be known as Beanie's, and it had stuck. A couple shot out the door, still slapping on their coats and scarves, the hubbub of the shop rolling out onto the pavement with them.

I caught the door, slipping inside. The heat hit me in a wave of coffee and gingerbread, which effectively masked the body odor of eighty people stuffed into space never meant to accommodate them.

Stripping my layers down, I peered around the line of customers for Suzy. She waved overhead in my direction from the counter piled high with takeaway cups and gift boxes without looking up, pointing to a vacant table amongst the throng congregating in the midst of her shop. I waved back though I knew she didn't see me and headed for the table, placing my keys on it at the same time as a coffee went down on the other side.

"Oh, I'm sorry, I thought the table was vacant—"

I looked up from the rough-looking hand that had a carved quality to it — not unusual in a person who worked on the land — straight into a pair of deep brown eyes that settled on me like a weighted blanket. I blinked, my words cutting off.

Shoulders broad enough to fill his yard shirt sat straight and even, tucked into a pair of dark jeans which showed a trim waist. His rust-tinted hair shimmered under the shop lights. But it was the impression of coiled energy under tight control that drew my attention.

"No. It's fine. I'll find somewhere else." The deep brown eyes never wavered from mine as he collected his cup from the tabletop and disappeared into the crowd before I could say anything more.

I blinked, wondering what just happened, but couldn't help searching the masses for his head of light-brown hair that reflected a hint of red beneath the store's lights.

I stood there, gaping mindlessly. Suzy appeared at my side. She untied her apron and tossed it onto the small table in a ball.

"It's as nippy as a pair of crickets in their underwear out there." She rapped the table, my keys rattling as she sank into the chair on the other side. I dragged my gaze from the crowd.

"Well, you have the heating in here high enough to entice a Sheik in." I grinned, leaning over to give her a hug. "Half the town must be here."

"You hear about the mess heading our way?"

"Which one?" I sipped my coffee. It scalded my tongue. "The cold front coming through that's predicted, or this earth-moving event everyone in White Cap seems to believe will bring the apocalypse?"

"The apocalypse. But we'll go with caffeine-saturated veins!"

I laughed. "I wouldn't have it any other way."

"And there's that murderer from the South trying to make it across the border in a big chase. Cops been around asking about it."

I raised my eyebrows; news like that would keep the town going until well after Christmas.

"You know we're well out of it all up at the ranch."

Being nearly two hours from a large town had its advantages. Our closest tiny town was White Cap — but with only a few thousand residents, it barely made a blip on the map.

Suzy shrugged. "Maybe you're safer up there. Got a pretty view, at least." She paused. "You hear anything from Black Hill?"

I bit my tongue, holding back everything I wanted to say. "No," I answered too fast. Suzy raised her eyebrows. "You know you're welcome at the ranch any time. I'll make a bed up for you at the big house."

"And leave this place in the hands of a few casual workers? They'd run the shop into the ground in a day or so."

"They can't be that bad."

"Only as bad as the trainer."

"Uh-huh." I sipped my drink, relishing real, barista-made coffee.

"I reckon I've seen just about everyone this week. Was wondering when you would make an appearance."

Coffee grits and what looked like flour covered the side of her black tee shirt. Her hair thrown up into a messy bun, Suzy has been blessed with slim shoulders that belayed the strength of the woman inside her small frame. A classical beauty in a country town was a rarity. Suzy's energy ran high at the best of times, but the festivities always gave her a boost that brought everyone else with her through the silly season to the other side.

"I'm here." I passed her the list. "Plus, the other things I messaged you about last week."

Suzy made short work of the list. "Not a problem. It's all out the back. Get one of the boys to help you get everything into that sexy truck of yours. Got a nice young man out there, too." She wiggled her eyebrows at me.

I grimaced, not taking her bait. "Becoming a cougar now? That's a step in the right direction."

Suzy wrinkled her nose at me as a waitress brought us two takeaway mugs of coffee. I took mine gratefully as I finished my first, the sweat that shivered out over my skin, not unwelcome after the biting conditions outside.

"You know I'll never take another partner—" She buried her face in her coffee. I reached across the table to grip her hand.

"And that's entirely your choice," I said firmly. "Archie was amazing. He was—"

"Irreplaceable." She hiccupped. I passed her a tissue from my coat. "It's only been four years, but I had him for nearly twenty. Golden years." She looked up at me, pinning me with eyes older than her barely-lined face suggested.

"I would wish the same for you, Eve. Golden days with a man who'll adore you."

I squeezed her hand back, my heart welling with emotion I couldn't put into words. "I'm sure it will happen one day."

"You need to look after yourself, Eve. There's more to life than your mountain and that ranch." Her grip fierce, I met her red-rimmed eyes.

"I've got some pretty deer. Maybe I'll catch myself a sexy cowboy." I grinned, but it fell flat under Suzy's assessing gaze.

"You'll need a whole lotta man for you, babe." She rose, untangling the strings of her apron. "Break's over. Get your stuff from the store. There's a box with your name on it. See you before Christmas?"

"I'll be back in," I promised, heading for the back of the shop, then paused, turning on my heel. "Are you alo– what are you doing for Christmas?" I rephrased my question. I asked every year, and each time, I hoped she'd say she'd come to the ranch. The thought of her alone in her cottage on the outskirts of town worried me.

"I'll do what I always do, Eve. Get the hell away from everyone, and have a quiet damned day to myself. A luxury." she promised me as I shook my head mournfully.

"Alright, go back to working your ass off," I grumbled, collecting my fresh coffee as I rose from the small table and reentered the throng.

The storeroom and office were at the back of the shop, but I had to wade through the crowd to get there. I skirted around people, the crowd in the long shop growing more raucous.

I slipped into the office, the white noise fading as I kicked the door shut. A headache niggled. I rubbed the top of my head, working my fingers to the hairline, no doubt messing my hair horribly. I had no idea how Suzy managed the place. The noise alone would kill me.

I wandered through the office and collected the box with all my printouts. Suzy had a brand spanking new laser cutting printer, which had been handy for branding with the ranch. She'd made me extra decals for the farm trucks and tons of promotional materials for shows and the sales yards.

I slipped back into the hall and headed for the storeroom, but a tall young man met me halfway, a box in his arms. He poked a handsome face around the edge of the box.

"You're Eve, right? Got a lot of stuff for uh— Red, uh, something..."

"Red Hart Ranch." I grinned back; his easy manner was contagious. "I can take it." I reached for the box. The boy — he couldn't have been much younger than me, maybe his early twenties — held on tight.

"Nu-uh. Boss lady'll have my hide. I'll follow you, ma'am."

"Alright..."

"Will. Will Kirk."

"Alright, Will Kirk. Let's go."

I led him back through the shop, waving to Suzy as I passed. "I'll be back in a day or so!" I yelled over the roar. She waved over her head again. I grinned, holding the door, and gestured Will to my truck.

He paused, turning in a circle. "Suz said you had a beast."

My lip curled. "My twin brother stole it for the day. Thinks it won't come back to bite him."

"Sounds like you have a lotta fun out there." His voice had a wistful note as he slid the box onto the passenger seat. I plopped my box below the passenger seat.

"Missing home?" I asked softly.

He jumped. "How'd you know?" he asked with a rueful smile.

"I was born here, Will Kirk. In a town of under three-thousand residents, chances are, I'm going to know most of them."

"Fair enough." He closed the door, his hands sliding into his pockets. His feet jiggled on the pavement.

"Did you grow up on the land?"

He nodded. "Yeah. Then I went to college. Wasn't for me. So, working my way around. Might try the PBR circuit." He mumbled to the ground.

"You're a bull rider?" I asked in surprise, taking stock of him, his muscle well hidden beneath his uniform shirt and pants.

"Did a bit for fun. Some drunken rides, too. Did okay." He shrugged.

"Well, you're welcome at Red Hart anytime you want an extra job if you're good with animals."

"Thanks, Ma'am." He tipped his head my way and headed back into Beanie's.

"You're welcome, Will." I shuffled my shopping around in the truck. He called me back.

"You hear about the big police chase through the state? Reckon they might close the border until New Year's. And there's that big snowstorm predicted."

"I heard about it. But don't put too much trust in everything Suz says. She loves a good piece of gossip, especially the earth-ending type."

"She a doomsday hoarder? A survivalist?"

"Only the worst in the North."

"Well, I don't mind a bit of gossip. Merry Christmas."

"Same to you." I smiled to myself as I got into the truck, knowing Suzy wouldn't mind me offering the young man a job.

A ripple ran across my shoulders as I leaned out to pull my door closed. The hinge creaked woefully. Forgetting I'd brought Trav's truck into town and not mine, I yanked on the door too hard. It didn't latch. Rust flaked to the road as I scrambled for the handle. Catching it as it bounced open again, I struggled with it for a moment, the keys sliding toward the edge of my leg.

Finally getting the door closed and sweating despite the icy air outside, I looked around the street for whatever had set off my spidey-sense.

Leaning against the wall next to the entrance to Beanie's was the same man who'd spoken to me inside the coffee shop, staring straight at me. His hair had a decidedly auburn tint to it. My gaze traced the strong lines of his jaw beneath a light shadow, the finest hint of silver peppered through it.

Covered with several day's growth, the ends of his hair touching the collar of his jacket, his jeans and worn boots form-fitting his lean, tall frame, he could have been a model for a men's clothing label. Not quite hard enough to be chiseled, his face had just enough angles to be striking.

I shook my head, breaking eye contact with him. Flustered, I thrust the key at the ignition, missing by miles, and dropped it on the floor of the cab. I recovered it, swearing to myself, glad the windows were up as some of my mom's church ladies walked by the truck. Waving, I managed to get the key in the ignition and crank the blasted thing, a miracle in itself.

I put the ancient truck in gear and chanced a glance back at Beanie's, sure I'd be staring at a blank wall. But the man still leaned against it, not completely out of place in the town, and still watching me. Our gazes caught, a jolt shooting through me. I fumbled the clutch, heat rising in my cheeks, and broke eye contact with him.

As I pulled away, I could swear I'd seen a hint of a smile on his face in the rearview mirror.

CHAPTER 2

An odd quiet settled over the ranch as the last of the hands traveled back to their family homes. Though the enormous tree got over-decorated with homemade ornaments and tinsel, Mom had still somehow found fresh poinsettias and sprayed half of them gold. The effect in the lounge was a magnificent spray of bright greens, reds, and golds.

The ranch had started out as full in early December. The snow was late this year, and we'd managed to get a lot more done during what should have been a time where the ranch wound down. Soon enough, the hands were giving us their farewells for the season — some who would return to the ranch year after year, and some we'd likely never see again.

It only took a few days, and in that week, the ranch grew steadily empty. Sitting at the foot of the mountain range, Red Hart Ranch sprawled over acres of prime land, deer and a few bison grazing in their respective fields.

The wildflowers that overpopulated the low hills in bursts of color were long gone with the onset of chill for the winter. However, the animals took little stock of the changes around them.

This herd was the largest we'd ever catered for, though the land could support more with ease. Travis wanted to expand the herd, but I loved how the ranch ran now: not overly busy but productive enough to keep the business flowing well while still looking after the land.

I placed my empty coffee mug on the table by the door, noting the absence of Jude's boots beneath it. Predictably, Travis hadn't gotten up yet, though the sun had risen an hour ago.

Even in midwinter, I couldn't stay asleep while the sun was up.

I crossed the open yard between the house and the barn, the movement loosening muscles cramped from a night checking on Dad. The weak sun on my face gave a glorious hint of warmth in the crisp morning air. Mixed with the woodsmoke from the night's dying fire inside the house, it encompassed everything I loved about this place.

Movement in the nearest field caught my eye, Jude's broad shoulders wrestling with something at ground level. Our foreman had opted to stay, one of a handful of workers who would see Christmas morning with us. Though Jude considered us family, he hadn't been back to visit his own in many years.

Wrangling a young deer born into the coldest part of the year, Jude had his back to me, engrossed in his own work. He looped his arm around the creature's thin neck while he checked its hooves and teeth, but the fawn didn't seem to be agreeable to his method.

Almost as tall as my brother, he stood a good six feet tall, his wide shoulders the perfect triangle shape for a cowboy, his shirt always tucked neatly into his jeans. When he wasn't rolling around on the ground, that is. Loose dirt kicked up, showering him in a rain of dark grains. He swore, long legs scrabbling for purchase. I loved having him around — loved having someone so trustworthy to work the animals, and besides, he was Trav's best friend — but I would also love to see him settle with someone.

I winced, remembering Suzy's constant pestering at the coffee shop over my own, non-existent love life, and resolved to keep my mouth firmly shut and my nose out of other people's lives.

"She's lively." I crouched beside Jude, just out of kicking distance of the scrambling week-old fawn. A hoof whistled past my nose. Apparently, I had misjudged the length of its legs. Or it had grown a lot overnight. The same hoof collected the foreman on the chin. He fell back with an *oof*, releasing his thrashing burden. The fawn lolloped off in search of its mother, nuzzling as he located her near the fence.

"Just a bit," Jude rubbed his chin ruefully as he rose and dusted himself off. "Good stock, though, Eve. She carries the bloodline well."

I smiled; the pairing of a mature breeding mother and a young buck had been my idea. "Good to know it worked. Do you have enough help this week? I can try to find some extra workers in town."

"Are you heading back again? My condolences." Jude grinned; it was common knowledge he hated leaving the ranch. Charismatic and energetic at home, he withdrew into himself when in public, becoming a hard shell of the kind-hearted man inside. "I'll be fine. I mean, if you find me someone with twenty years' experience, I'll take it with the snow predicted, but don't go on a unicorn hunt for me. Not at this time of year."

I nodded, "Well, if you're sure." I thought of Will at Beanie's. "I might have someone for you in the new year, though."

"Always welcome." Jude's fingers tapped a quick rhythm on his belt. I took a step back, giving him the space he needed.

"I'll leave you to it, then." I looked around the open area, but nothing seemed to need work.

"Appreciate it."

Spotting the short roofline of the cabins hidden in the treeline, I began to plan how I'd fill my morning. The bunkhouses hadn't been checked for a while, and now that over half the cowboys had left for the season, I had time to check things were still in order across the ranch.

Having made my decision, I turned back to Jude, but the foreman was already engrossed in tightening hinges on the barn door. I left him to his solitary work and hiked up into the low hills.

The long drive back into town looming, I wanted to spend as much time as I could outside. By the time I reached the treeline, my legs were warm. Ready to ditch my coat, I knew the icy air creeping down the mountain had a sharp bite to it. I'd have to deal with the warmth or risk the chill seeping into my bones.

I knocked on the door to the bunkhouse, not keen to disturb one of the younger men, but I needn't have worried; the place was empty. And surprisingly clean. Every evening I made sure we fed everyone at the big house, and most nights, the hands stayed up with us for a few hours before they fell into their own beds.

Without a town around for entertainment, we formed a community of sorts, tucked away at the edge of the borderlands.

After hunting around their spartan kitchen and lounge area with little to do, I left for the lone cabin on the other side of the big house, set further back. The original shack had been on the property for years. Travis and Jude refit it with modern plumbing and wiring one offseason. Now it only came into use when we had an excess of staff or during breeding times and the sale season.

My chest opened with the walk, allowing deeper breaths in. I rolled my shoulders, relishing the stretch, and inhaled through my nose. The forest filled my senses, all sharp pine needles, and earthy warmth. Faint in the cooler air, but it dredged up memories of Trav and me racing around the forest as kids before the first snow.

Stepping up onto the short verandah of the old cabin, I reached under the hollowed-out window frame, hoping I wouldn't encounter anything with eight legs and fangs. I flicked upward, and the key fell into my palm.

The cabin was just as we'd left it. We'd never had a problem with vandalism and got few people this far from anywhere. The worst squatters we had to worry about were a few birds and cheeky squirrels, maybe the occasional badger. Inside, it smelled musky, though someone had collected a basket of pinecones and stacked the small rack with dry firewood.

Giving the place a once over, I locked it up, replaced the key in its home, and headed back to the house to collect yet another list of supplies.

While my order from Beanie's had been plenty for the ranch's business needs over Christmas, Mom had forgotten a stack of things, more than doubling the original list she'd given me. I thought about her the whole way into town, music playing softly through my car stereo system forgotten for the most part.

Mom had taken on a lot more than she usually did; the stress of seeing her husband on his back for the first time in over forty years had driven her anxiety levels through the roof. Trav and I had our own concerns, but we kept them to ourselves, not wanting to add to her stress.

With most of the farmhands heading home to whatever families they had, we were short-staffed if anything went wrong. And with the reports of weather closing in on the North, we were right in its path.

"New drifter in town," Suzy murmured as she placed my coffee on top of the bunch of parcels, balancing it with such care, it could have been an art form.

I shifted slightly, hoping the ham wouldn't take a slide south of my hips. Suzy topped the lot off with a neatly-folded ham bag. I rolled my eyes, taking a careful step around customers clamoring for the few staff's attention. Beanie's patrons filled the place to the brim, just as busy as the few days prior, with the addition of carols barring over the roar of conversations where everyone yelled above each other to be heard.

I smiled my gratitude for the coffee, though I doubted she could see it.

"Yeah? You know we open the ranch up each Christmas. Jude said he could use someone with experience. Oh, I offered Will a job. Are you mad at me?"

Suzy laughed. "Hell no, I'm not mad. I'm glad you did. Boy is wasted around here. He'll suit the ranch."

"Send him up when things quiet down."

"I got you, babe. Now, about this other man..."

I sighed, shaking my head. She'd never give up. "Fine," I grumbled, "Send him my way," I spoke around a mouthful of ham bag.

"She did."

"Oh eff—" I jumped at the gravelly voice behind me, my coffee teetering as I tried to realign everything with varying degrees of success. Wrapping my arms around the whole lot, I leaned into the ham and waited to wear my scalding hot coffee.

"Whoa. Sorry." The trembling coffee disappeared from my hands before it cascaded over me, the ham liberated from my arms. Suddenly left with little to hold, I stared at my rescuer.

Dark, sparkling eyes surveyed me.

In a swift move that made my balancing skills look pathetic, he hefted the ham in one arm, placed the coffee on top, and grabbed the bag with the turkey. I blinked as the coffee reappeared in my hand. Suzy disappeared discreetly into a knot of customers.

"Um, thank you?" I smiled at the same man I'd seen the last time I'd come into town, clutching a pair of breadsticks over my chest.

His reddish-brown hair curled at the neck of his jacket, though in this light, his stubble appeared a touch darker. Dark brown eyes that still managed to sparkle with internal humor were set into a face both rugged and intense. His eyes alone gave a hint of the man inside. Heat crawled up my cheeks in a slow flush. I must have resembled a thermometer in the height of a July day.

"I'll never get between a woman and her coffee. I do want to live." He grinned, shifting Red Hart's Christmas fare to his side, extending his hand. "Rhys Archer."

"Eve Beaumont." I proffered two fingers around my remaining burden. He squeezed them gently with calloused fingers, his eyes never leaving mine. A thrill ran along my arm, settling somewhere in my stomach. "You said Suzy sent you over?"

"She did. Where's your truck?"

My brow dipped, but a smile crept across my lips. "This way." I led him out the doors where he managed to grab his hat from the rack on the wall, calling goodbyes over my shoulder to Suzy.

I headed down the street toward my truck, stopping when I realized he hadn't followed me. "Truck's this way." I nodded to my F350, freshly washed, the badging gleaming in the late morning sun.

"That's not what you were driving the other day." He hefted the ham into the cooler.

I put everything else in the small fridge in the bed. His hand brushed mine as we grabbed at the fridge lip together. A shiver ran over the back of my hand. I withdrew it quickly, dropping my eyes for a moment.

"My brother stole my truck when you last saw me. Typical." I grinned, squeezing my empty hands together.

"I don't blame him. Beautiful." He patted the side of my truck, but his eyes never left mine. My skin flared with sensation even though it wasn't me he touched. Archer — as I had deemed him already — cleared his throat. I refused to use full names for the people I knew wouldn't be staying on with us for a long period, and this man was clearly in that camp. Though for some reason, it gave me a pang low in my chest. "When she said you owned the ranch up on the mountain, I figured you'd be a practical person." Archer finished packing everything away and tapped the side of my truck. "That's it. Have a Merry Christmas, Eve."

He tipped his hat — actually tipped it — and turned away, heading back along Main Street.

How often does a girl meet a man with manners like that? I stared after him with an unattractive open mouth, and my brain kicked into gear.

"Wait," I called. "Didn't Suzy tell you we have an open-door policy for Christmas?"

He turned slowly on his heel, one broad shoulder tensing beneath his jacket. "She might have mentioned it."

"Do you have somewhere to spend Christmas, Archer?"

He shook his head. "No. I didn't want to assume."

"Well, consider yourself invited." I opened the passenger door to my truck and walked around to the driver's side without checking if he'd followed me.

"Where are you from?" I asked, waiting to see if my prediction came true.

Archer opened his mouth, sent me a quick, sideways look, and snorted. "You already know what I'm going to say."

"Heard it a thousand times before." I squeezed the steering wheel, wondering if I'd let a pretty face talk me into coming home with me. I turned the thought over for a moment, but nothing about Archer sat poorly with me.

Not that that was proof of anything.

"Is it a big place, this ranch of yours?" He asked, leaning back with his eyes closed. The slope of his shoulders dipped just enough to be noticeable, and I suspected he hadn't felt comfortable enough to relax in some time.

"My parents, not mine," I corrected. "And yes, it's a decent size."

When I didn't get a response, I took my eyes off the road to chance a look at Archer. Head tipped back, auburn hair flopped over the side of his face, he snored softly. Something in my heart tugged; I'd grown up on the ranch and never not had a place to call home.

The life of a drifter was about as far from my life experience as the moon — I couldn't fathom the loneliness Archer must deal with, that total lack of stability. The absence of a safe place to close his eyes, to rest.

I smiled, turning the music up a little, and let him sleep.

A large, wooden sign covered in our red and white branding proclaimed the entrance to Red Hart Ranch. Planted beside a large set of farm gates, they were wide enough to get a cattle truck through. I pulled in just as Trav approached from the other side in his truck, a large cut tree poking above the cab, its branches hanging forlornly over the dented bed.

I rolled my eyes. We had sufficient trees of our own, but every year, Travis insisted on cutting one from the local vet's property, an hour across the edge of the mountain range. He spent a lot of time choosing the perfect tree, though I suspected it wasn't the flora that drew him to Rachel's property.

Archer shifted, stretching. He looked at me sideways, an eyebrow quirked.

"Boyfriend?"

"Twin. You don't need to look so worried."

He snorted as we trundled along the drive, waiting for the dust Trav kicked up to clear. I kept an eye on Archer, knowing the scenery drew the eye. Everyone who came to the ranch

41

had a similar reaction. The Montana mountains were stunning at any time, but there was something about Red Hart that always took your breath away — no matter how long you'd been around it.

He stared pensively out the passenger window, seeming to sink deeper into himself until the house came into view, and his jaw actually dropped.

I hid a grin under the pretense of tucking my hair behind my ears and pulled into the parking bay Dad had carved out for us, back when he could work the tractor.

Archer shook his head, taking it all in.

"You've been here for a while, huh?"

I nodded. "The house started life as a log cabin some hundred and fifty plus years ago, one of the first on the border up here. The Beaumonts came down from Canada and settled as an early incarnation of customs agents, apparently. Lawmen and all." I wiggled my eyebrows at him.

Archer jerked and gripped the door handle tight, white spreading over roughened knuckles. I frowned as he wordlessly hoisted himself out of the cab without a backward glance.

Opening my own door, I swung my five-and-half-foot frame straight into my brother.

"Give a girl some room," I grumbled at him, hoisting bags from the bed. "And maybe next year, choose a tree from one of the million we have here?" My snark came out to play, but something had set me on edge. I sent Trav a quick grin to soften my words.

"Spitfire." He poked me in the back of the knees with his boot. I reached into the bed and hefted the turkey at him with both hands, relieved when he caught it, or Mom would be roasting something else for Christmas.

"Probably." I caught movement behind him, and for a moment, I thought Archer had come around to help unload, but when I turned back, he was still on the other side of the truck, his hands wrapped around the ham. I peered behind Trav. "Who's that?"

Travis grinned. "I could ask you the same thing."

"Drifter," we both blurted at the same time, laughing.

"Seriously? Well, it's not like we don't have the room since most everyone has gone home for the season."

"Those that have a home." I waved to Jude, the tall cowboy lounging against the verandah's timber post, dressed in his trademark duster jacket. A coffee thermos sat comfortably in his hand. I'd rarely seen him without it. "Jude's been here long enough to be a permanent fixture."

"Yeah, he's never going to leave. Eve, this is Simon Haldon. He's been working a few of the ranches down south and thought he'd try for work along the border for a change of scenery," Trav introduced his drifter, catching my eye. The corner of his mouth crooked up.

I smiled at the man behind Trav politely. *A change of scenery* often meant a cowboy had worn out their welcome. A crisp, dark blue shirt tucked neatly into a fresh pair of black jeans; his lean frame met my brother's six-foot-two height. I surveyed him with a critical eye, wondering what he'd done.

He winked, a cheeky grin spreading across his face.

Or who.

Most likely, he'd tried to seduce the last ranch owner's daughter. Well, good luck to him with that here. His smile was infectious, though, and I couldn't help grinning back as I shook his long-fingered hand. He held on a moment too long, releasing me almost reluctantly.

"Rhys Archer. Nobody from Nowhere, apparently." I waved to my passenger, a small doubt blooming in my stomach. Trav had obviously done his homework, and I'd offered two men jobs without doing a single background check.

A little hard to do when you knew nothing about one of them.

Archer caught my eye, the hint of a smile tugging at the corner of my lips, and the seed died.

He nodded to Trav, hefting the ham.

I rolled my eyes at the ambiguity of their stories; would these guys ever become original? Always the same sob story. A broken heart, or broken too many; someone they'd conflicted with. Often the foreman or ranch owner. Those cowboys never lasted long, as they couldn't take direction and usually couldn't do the job required well.

Occasionally it was theft, cattle rustling, or something more personal. Sometimes, abuse, though those were rarer, at least, for us. I'd heard horror stories from other ranches, but so far, we'd managed to keep our own free of troubles.

Still, additional hands were welcome when we were on a skeleton crew, and extra company over Christmas never hurt, either.

I turned to Archer, but he stared over my head, his hard gaze locked on Simon. I frowned, looking between them. Simon stilled, holding the shorter man's gaze, his shoulders a tight line beneath the crisp shirt. A muscle jumped in his jaw, and I had the impression of his discomfort under Archer's scrutiny.

Gravel crunched behind me. Archer strode toward the house, a single bag over one shoulder, the ham tucked under the other.

Travis tapped my shoulder. "Do they know each other?"

"I have no idea." I gripped a bag of supplies and headed up to the house while my brother and his passenger unloaded the tree, my eyes fixed on my own drifter.

Who are you, Rhys Archer?

CHAPTER 3

I followed Archer's shadow to the main house, leaving the other two chattering away as they hauled the tree after us. Striding up the few wide steps to the main house, he knocked on the door with his elbow before I could catch up to him. Jude had disappeared off the verandah.

"I'll get it." I reached around him, fiddling with the latch with two fingers and finally getting it to open. "Mom's probably upstairs with Dad. She won't hear us," I apologized.

Archer raised an eyebrow. I shuffled forward with effort, the turkey wet and gooey in my arms, despite being wrapped in plastic. The thing weighed a ton. Condensation ran over my fingers while my stomach balked at the bird juice dripping from them.

"Dad's laid up in bed. He had a– a turn," I shrugged, "a stroke. A few weeks back. A doctor saw him initially, but he won't let us take him into town to see a specialist and refuses to let us call one in. I'm scared he's getting worse." I clamped my mouth shut, biting my lips in the process. "Sorry. You didn't need to know all that."

Archer wedged his boot across the door and motioned me inside. "It's okay, Eve. If I'm going to live here, it's good to know. Thank you."

I blinked at his soft tone, edging around him into the house. He followed me inside, kicking off his boots at the door though I left mine on.

"Uh– you can put that...on the bench. There." I motioned where I wanted the ham and placed the turkey in the sink. "The bunkhouse is just off to the right if you want to put your things somewhere. You can see it from the verandah. Or there's the cabin just on the rise to the back of the house if you'd like your own space? There's a path," I added belatedly. Realizing Archer had to be at least ten years older than most of the hands and possibly wouldn't be as keen as Simon to share his evenings with a bunch of rowdy farmhands. The younger-looking drifter should fit in well with them if he got along with my twin.

"Thanks."

"I can take you up there if you want to wash up—" I looked up from sorting the melting bird in the sink, but he'd already disappeared out the door. Travis and Simon dragged the tree through the doorway and got stuck. "—if you like."

I sighed, shaking my head as Travis shrugged, mouthing *"what?"* at me.

"We can make it," Trav called over the top of the copious amounts of greenery. I assumed Simon stood on the other side, his reply muffled behind the branches.

The boys counted it down and hauled the tree through the door, where it exploded in a shower of pine needles. Two proud faces peered at me through the doorway. I blinked as the pine lumbered through the house, towed by my brother and his drifter, leaving me staring at the mess in the entrance foyer of Red Hart Ranch.

I was glad I hadn't taken my boots off.

By the time I'd cleaned up the mess the boys had made in the foyer, listening to them debate the finer points of tree husbandry, their chatter had overloaded. Red Hart could be a busy place, but usually, I had the house to myself.

Patting the turkey's wrapping dry, I carried it to the long deep freezer at the end of the butler's pantry behind the kitchen. It might seem like a luxury, but with the number of people we fed, it quickly became necessary.

Washing my hands in the sink, my arms finally free of bird, I turned and ran into Simon.

"Oh, hell." I stepped back in a hurry, dropping the hand towel. Simon bent to retrieve it for me, his hand lingering on mine. "Thanks."

His grey gaze swept me from head to toe. "Just wanted to see how you were doing. If you needed any help," he clarified, leaning against the doorframe with his ankles crossed, completely barring my way out of the pantry.

"I was working," I said pointedly but smiled. "Uh, in that direction." I motioned around him, but he didn't move.

"Also wanted to say thanks for letting me into your home. It must be odd, having strangers around." His arms folded over his chest, a grin spread over his face.

I opened my mouth to say I had no problem with it, then closed it again. He'd know that, as a regular cowboy. I wondered again briefly why he'd left his last job and decided to put that baby to rest.

"Simon, we have new cowboys here all the time. Hands come and go. As long as you stand by the house rules and work well with Jude, you won't have a problem."

I stepped around him. He caught my elbow to stop me before I made it into the kitchen. I looked down at his hand and back to his face.

I don't need to ask you why you left the last ranch, do I?

I put the question in my eyes so I wouldn't have to ask, but also so he'd get the point. A smile spread over his lips, his eyes alight. I laughed, shaking my head as I pulled away. "Thank you for bringing in the tree."

Great. Now he thinks of me as a challenge.

"Anything to help."

I'll bet.

Geez, I needed to reign in that snark before it got out of control. Rolling my eyes at myself and at Simon, I set up a roast and veggies for dinner. Spruce garlands gave a sharp tang over the top of everything, a constant reminder of the season.

Fortunately, Simon returned to helping Trav, but I felt his eyes on me a few times. I kept my head down, biting my lips. What made his attention different from others'? Almost every new cowboy made a pass at me, with Travis and Jude championing my choice not to be involved with any of them.

This time, something felt different, and I couldn't quite put my finger on it. Boiling the kettle, I made a pot of tea and took two heated cups up the stairs. Peering into my parent's room at the top of the stairs, I paused. Both were asleep on the bed. Dad lay under the covers, Mom bedside him, fully dressed and half-sitting with a book fallen closed on her lap. I placed the pot gently on the bedside stand and left the room quietly.

I walked slowly down the stairs, Travis and Simon bantering about sports. On a whim, I set another batch of mulled wine on the stovetop, clearing up as I hailed the boys setting the tree upright.

"Trav, please look after this while I'm out?
Don't let it spoil like the last batch."

Travis waved over his shoulder at me.
Biting my lip, I looked between the stove and
the tree, wondering if I shouldn't have started
making it at all. I glanced over my shoulder.
Trav had disappeared around the tree, but
Simon caught my eye.

"I'll look after it for you," he called with a
small wave, laughing at the mistrust I couldn't
hide. "Go, do whatever you're going to do. It'll
be fine. I'll add something from a favorite
recipe in there. A little personal touch." He
winked.

I got the impression he was capable of not
allowing it to over boil and nodded, still
cautious but less so than I had been with it
under my brother's attention.

Dusk closed in with a distinctly icy edge.
Stars began to pop out in the twilight, twinkling
in a clear sky. Despite the temperate weather, I
sensed the changes at the foot of the mountain.
Even with only one door open, the early
evening air filtered in, calling me to leave the
confines of the house.

Leaving Travis to argue with Simon, who slipped into ranch life as though he'd always been here, I grabbed my jacket from the coat rack at the door. I opted to leave my hat off, unraveling my hair from its tight ponytail as I hiked into the low foothills behind the house.

Instinct told me Archer would choose the cabin; something about him said he wasn't the *sharing* type of guy.

I waved to Jude still on the tractor, showing some of the newer hands who'd opted to stay on for the season how to use the old beast's snowplow. He waved back, no irritation showing on his tanned face. He had more patience than any man I knew. If nothing else, the time with a skeleton crew wouldn't be wasted in hours of training and upskilling.

Dusk fell early, inch by inch, the sky dropping to the tops of the fir trees that overpopulated the low hills behind the house. Above them, the mountain stretched out, little of its heavily treed side visible in the falling light, though its white cap stood out against the darkening sky.

By the time I reached the cabin, lights were glowing from inside. I hesitated, wondering if I wasn't overstepping into his privacy — Archer clearly valued his. I inhaled a sharp breath and knocked.

He opened it quickly, still pulling a shirt over his head. A well-muscled torso flashed at me, tight ridges carved into his body. Heat rose in my cheeks as he pulled the material to the waist of his jeans, covering the defined vee that led into them.

Archer's eyes settled on me. Dark and assessing, they bore right through me.

"I just wanted to invite you to the house for dinner," I blurted. "I figured you wouldn't have much food in that bag, and I didn't want you to starve. I've put a roast on — oh God, please tell me you're not a vegetarian. Not that there's anything wrong with that." I snapped my mouth shut before I rambled further.

Something about him flustered me, the way he looked at me, or just his presence in general. I knew I would never be able to keep a secret from this man — not that I had anything to hide

— and determined to keep my distance from him.

So why am I standing in his doorway while he gets dressed?

My cheeks burned again. I resisted the urge to fidget beneath his gaze. His intense gaze had a sparkle to it, and I knew I'd been caught perving. Which made the heat in my cheeks all the worse.

"Do I look like a vegetarian?" he asked mildly, stepping aside to wave me in. I hesitated for a second; though I'd checked the cabin this morning — *hell, was that only this morning?* — the cabin suddenly seemed like his own place.

"No?" I asked, shrugging my jacket off. I laid it across my hands, clenching them tightly together. "We live on a ranch. There really aren't many vegetarians around. Though I'm sure, it's a solid dietary choice."

"Not much of a thing where I'm from, either."

I bit my lip, wanting badly to ask where *from* was for this man, but I knew he wouldn't answer. I caught the glimmer in his eye as he recognized I wouldn't push him and wandered further into the small cabin. His duffle bag lay open on the small coffee table set in front of the worn, two-seater couch.

"I'm sorry about the sofa. We keep going to replace it, but hardly anyone stays up here. I– I just thought it would suit you better, away from everyone else–" My mouth ran on as I cringed at myself internally. Archer's hands on my shoulders stopped me.

Stopped everything, in fact.

My breath hitched as his body warmth soaked into my shoulders. His fingers curled gently around the tops of my arms, pressing gently.

"Eve. The place is fine. Much better than what I've been sleeping in, believe me." The corner of his mouth quirked as he studied me.

A shiver rippled up my spine. Opening his mouth like he wanted to say more, he dropped hands, tearing his gaze from mine.

Cold air wrapped my shoulders in the absence of his hands. I shivered again; this tingle was different from the previous one. Archer turned his back to me, running a hand over his hair. Autumn shades crisscrossed the back of his head, the longer strands curling around the nape of his neck.

I turned in a circle, casting about for something to break the strained silence. My gaze fell on a small knife with a decorative blade on the coffee table, an embroidered brown blanket folded neatly beneath it.

"Do you carve?" I guessed wildly, clenching my jacket. Despite my discomfort, I didn't have the desire to race out the door away from him.

Archer turned, focusing on where I gestured to the coffee table. "Yes." He leaned down, collecting the small knife, turning it in his hand. I studied the calluses on the palm of his hand.

"Something you've always done?"

"My father taught me. I've made things — animals, mostly— since I was a teenager. He wouldn't let me try any younger than that."

"In case you nipped the tops of your fingers off." I nodded. "Dad and Travis were the same. But my brother still bears the scars. They bled so much," I said with a short laugh.

Archer grinned in commiseration. "They do." He wiggled his own fingers, the tips covered with faint lines, stains etched into them. He grimaced. "Last town I was in, I did some work as a mechanic. Promise, I do wash up. Sometimes."

"A jack of all trades." I drew my eyes from his hand to his face, tracing the few days growth there, the lines of concentration across his forehead, but not those of stress I usually saw in a younger drifter's face. I tapped his hand. "You are an enigma, Rhys Archer."

"Nah, just a country boy."

"From...?" I pushed, raising an eyebrow.

"It's elk horn. The handle." Archer tipped the small knife into my hand. "Careful. I sharpened it a few days ago. Thought I might try carving something tonight."

I nodded, running my hands over the yellow and black etchings, worn smooth with time and use.

"Will you come down to the house for dinner?"

"Let me wash up." He waved his grease-etched hands at me.

I nodded, taking the hint, and waited outside, pulling my jacket back over my shoulders. Dragging my almost-waist-length dark hair past the collar, I let it hang untamed down my back, regretting not at least getting a beanie before I left the house.

In ten quick minutes, the ranch house's lights showed over the treeline where the cabin stood above it. The cold sank against my skin in the night air, and I berated myself for being so wimpy.

Archer came through the cabin doorway with his hat in his hand. He slid his feet into well-worn but expensive boots outside the door, pulling it closed behind him. I studied them, not game to look at his face, the same longing to know more about him but something that edged on intimidation next to it.

Telling myself not to be so ridiculous, I took a step back, watching him. His movements were sure. He didn't appear to be uncomfortable with me around, which meant he *was* used to people, regardless of what he told me otherwise. Which wasn't much. With a start, I realized that Archer said little about himself and let his clothes and outward persona tell a story that might not be entirely true.

Who are you, Rhys Archer?

The question echoed in my head for the second time. I had the inkling it wouldn't be the last.

He locked up with the key, slipping it back into its hidey-hole. "You don't have much of a problem with strangers up here, do you?" He looked almost wistful. I fell into step with him, trailing back to the house, blazing with light — a beacon in the foothills.

"We're too far from most places, and the border really isn't an issue. You'd have to traverse the mountain to get anywhere." I jerked my head back to the mountain, which gave Red Hart such a famous backdrop. "Where are you from?"

Archer sent me an amused sideways glance. "It's nice to be away from everything. All the chatter of the town," he said softly, still looking at me.

"The house might be a busy place tonight," I warned with a smile. "I left because of the noise. The boys yapping away." I remembered I hadn't seen Mom for a bit and promised myself I'd check on her before dinner. "And I'll introduce you to Jude. He's our foreman," I added to his raised eyebrows.

"Your brother doesn't take care of everything?"

"Oh, he does, but he's no good with the staff. No patience. Jude turned up when he was fourteen, one summer and never left. Sort of a fixture."

"You've created a home for the people here." Archer stopped on the rise just above the house. A line of workers trickled in through the front doors.

"Not me. It's just... how the place feels, I guess." When I turned back to him, he wasn't looking at the house anymore.

"Eve, I—" He broke off, slapping his hand to the pocket of his jeans. A faint jingle of Frankie Lane's *Dead Man's Hand* filled the forest around us. "Dammit."

I raised an eyebrow. "I didn't know they made ringtones that old."

Archer shot me a hard look, smirking, and pulled out his phone. He gave me an apologetic one-shouldered shrug and answered the call.

Already missing the warmth of his presence, I walked down to the house on my own.

I thought you were going to stay away from this man.

I knew I could argue with my head all night but having someone to talk to who hadn't been around for the last decade or so made a nice change. Most of the drifters and cowboys who came through were either players, finding a pretty girl at every ranch, or so used to their

66

own company they could barely hold a conversation with anyone else at all.

Archer was neither of those.

The rumble of conversation inside the house reached me. I hesitated at the corner of the verandah, hidden in the shadow of the north-facing wall. After the quiet of the walk, having only spent time with Archer, I suddenly didn't want to go back into the house.

"Eve."

I turned too fast, cricking my neck. Archer stood behind me, his hand outstretched as though he would touch me. My skin tingled in response, even as he dropped his hand.

"Quick call."

"Yeah," Archer sighed, stuffing his hand into his pocket. "Just an old friend."

A friend from where?

Stop prying into other people's lives, Eve.

He gave me a quick grin, stepping up to the verandah. He held out a hand. I took it, his rough fingers curling around mine as he tugged me up beside him. As we stepped into the light, he released my hand with a quick squeeze that lifted my stomach to somewhere in the vicinity of my chest.

Or maybe it was my heart.

Do NOT fall for a drifter.

My head berated my heart, but one of them wasn't listening.

CHAPTER 4

Though the ranch held less than half its regular occupants, the big house filled quickly with its usual chatter and laughter. Something about this time of year always brought the hands in for longer each night, staying to keep us company, or maybe it was the other way around. Despite that, we were all exhausted and doing more jobs than usual.

Archer had helped me wind tiny fairy lights through the garlands above the doorway and windows, adding a festive glow to the house.

I smiled over the heads at the table; plates empty, the racks of ribs I'd put into the double oven the barest of bones remaining. I doubted I'd manage to make a decent stock from them, but I'd try. Our late-winter vegetable harvest had yielded some great root vegetables, and I wanted to use what we had.

Dad sat at the top of the table in his customary seat, Mom perched on the corner next to him, gripping his hand. He sipped a glass of whiskey with a trembling hand, Mom watching him with sharp, albeit tired eyes. He picked at his food. I didn't mind, glad to see him out of his bed and willing to socialize. Travis sat on his other side, Jude and Archer across from him.

"Who brought Dad downstairs?" I murmured to Jude, passing him a fresh beer. He grinned his thanks, swallowing an enormous mouthful of roasted vegetables.

"Thank Archer. Trav and I were talking about it, and by the time we'd made up our minds...we walked in, and here was Len and Betty listening to this guy," he elbowed Archer in the ribs, "regaling them with stories about cattle running wild through a town. And a few other things."

The drifter flinched but didn't raise his head, though his shoulders shifted beneath his shirt.

Jude rolled one shoulder, looking just as uncomfortable as Archer had a moment ago. He rubbed the shadow over his chin. Travis shot me a look as I opened my mouth; I closed it, slightly confused. I hesitated a moment then opened it again.

"Thank you," I gave Archer's shoulder a squeeze. To my surprise, he reached up to cover my hand, pressing gently.

"Never gonna be a problem. Though I could use some help hefting the big fella back up there tonight." He raised his beer to cheers Dad, who gave him a lopsided grin back.

I blinked back tears, my hand tightening on Archer's shoulder. My fingers soaked into the warmth of his back. I stepped back, but that same warmth traveled up my arm, despite breaking contact with him.

My thanks lodged in my throat, I busied myself with dinner, hoping we could make it through the Christmas season without any more tragedies.

Dinner passed as a speedy affair; when you're feeding a long table full of cowboys, there's not usually a lot of leftovers.

I smiled as I leaned past Archer and Jude deep into a debate over tractor engines. Both were somewhat clean while still managing to be a bit dirty from the day's work, despite having apparently washed up.

Clean shirts, clean boots, and a quick wash before you came up to the big house for a meal, Red Hart had held to the tradition for years, and I saw no reason to change it.

Collecting their plates, I twisted, hooking the water jug on my fingers, determined to make as fewest trips back to the island bench as possible.

I straightened, taking a wobbly step backward as a buttoned shirt that smelled brand new stepped in front of me.

"Wow, that's a very clean shirt, Simon. Um. Well done?" I offered a small smile, still remembering the pass he'd made at me in the kitchen.

"Only the best for a lady." His smooth smile sent alarm bells ringing as he liberated the plates from my hands. I heard a small snicker behind me and kicked Jude's chair.

"Thank you," I said politely. "Maybe some of us could take your example." I snuck a cheeky look over my shoulder. Jude made a lewd gesture with his hand, Travis laughing out loud across the table. I kicked out again and got Archer by mistake.

"Oh, shit. Sorry," I apologized when he *ooffed*. "That was aimed at someone else." I mock-glared at Jude.

"Watch out, Archer, she's formidable with those boots. We've nearly lost her foot up our asses on many occasions." Travis looked woefully at his plate. I tossed a half-eaten bread roll at him.

Archer leaned back, his eyes laughing at me as I leaned past him. My collar grew hot, and I was glad to excuse myself to the kitchen.

Simon collected more plates, helping me clean up.

"Sit down," I waved him away. "I've got this."

Simon leaned over the edge of the counter, across the only cleared space. "If you've got nothing planned for afterward, I thought I'd..." He trailed off, looking at his interlaced hands.

My breath caught. Not pausing in my clean up, I glanced at him sideways. "Thought you'd what?" I asked lightly.

He grinned, turning sideways to look up at me. "I thought I might make dessert." His eyes burned into mine, and I knew he'd set that up to sound like something else.

Testing the waters.

My brain protested that indulging him *wasn't* a good idea. I ignored it.

"What did you have in mind?"

"Have you got more of that red wine we used to make up the spiced batch before?"

I grinned. "*We* didn't do anything. *You* made something amazing. But if I could watch what you did....?" I let the question hang, giving him the opportunity to keep the secret to himself. His broad smile said everything.

"I'd love to."

"Then, you're welcome to help me clean this up, and I'll make you some space."

Simon worked comfortably beside me, far better than I had expected. Occasionally, I felt the eyes of the others on me. Both Jude and Travis knew I rarely socialized outside of our tight circle. Rarely with the staff — Jude the exception, as he counted more as family than anything else.

My neck prickled under the attention of a man I wasn't used to. I kept my head down, chatting quietly to Simon. My heartbeat picked up every time I felt Archer's gaze on me, working through Simon's instructions and learning a few skills and tips along the way.

Soon the place smelled of Christmas: cinnamon, cloves, orange zest, and a few star anise Simon dug from the depths of the spice cabinet. Chatter and laughter filled the house. Rowdier from the boys, though Dad's new laugh-cough still gripped my chest every time.

"Glad he's down here?" Simon stirred the enormous pot that held several bottles of wine, rich aroma rising from within its depths, incredibly evocative. I knew I would remember this Christmas forever.

I nodded, wiping a hand over my face, and pretending to push back sweat. Simon pretended not to see my tears.

"Yep," I whispered, then cleared my throat. "After the past few weeks, it's so good to know we're not having a lonely Christmas. I thought the house might be a bit..."

"Empty." Simon gave me a sidelong look, nudging my shoulder.

I nodded. Simon offered me the spoon. "Ten this way then another ten counterclockwise," he grinned.

"Sure you're not just overly OCD?" I joked.

Simon's eyes darkened, the humor leaving them. "Something like that."

He spun on his heel, facing the chopping board. Handfuls of herbs were laid out in perfect lines across the thick slab of maple inlaid with darker walnut.

His hand wrapped around the handle of my largest kitchen knife, slicing with precise movements. I watched, mesmerized by his rhythm, stirring the mulled wine without really looking.

Hairs rose on my arms. I stopped stirring, looking past Simon to the long table. Archer's dark gaze caught mine. Heavy, assessing, but not invasive. Warmth ran up my chest and into my cheeks.

The room disappeared around me, narrowing to just Archer's face. I studied him in return: the heavy brow, dark, liquid eyes I could fall into, the sculpted jaw with several days' growth. My fingers itched to touch it, to feel the rough texture, wondering what it would feel against my bare skin.

Said skin flushed hotter. Hands suddenly wrapped around mine, wrenching the spoon from my grasp.

I blinked at Simon, whirling around me. The saucepan was pulled away from me, set on the heavy wooden bench as he muttered to himself. A whole nutmeg bobbed on the surface, caught in an eddy of spiced wine.

The chatter of the room returning full force, I ran a hand over my hair.

My eyes flew back to Archer, who held my gaze for a single second, the corners of his mouth hinting at a smile before he turned back to something Jude said, his shoulders shaking with laughter.

A shadow shifted, blocking my view of the table. Simon's face replaced Archer's, his grey eyes a storm of emotion. "You need to keep your attention on what you're doing, Eve," he rebuked lightly, his tone not matching the emotion roiling across his face.

He took a step closer, his face clearing of emotion, becoming a little harder, a little colder. I shivered, wrapping my arms around myself, despite the heat of the kitchen, backing into the bench behind me.

"Sorry, I got... sidetracked," I offered, not daring to take my eyes off the man in front of me.

His lips curled in something of half a smile and half a sneer. "I thought you didn't do the locals, Eve. The boys had a laugh about it after a few beers the other night, such a straight woman, all rules and no bend. Or was that a lie?"

My stomach clenched at the thought of being a topic of conversation in the bunkhouse, and I wished for a moment I'd sent Archer there. Perhaps he would have stopped the talk. It wasn't that I didn't expect them not to do it, but I was surprised it had been said so blatantly to my face.

His eyes drew an icy line from my face to my waist and back, though the return journey was much more languid.

The sneer became his easy smile, so much more him, and a little of the ice left my arms. I stepped around him, but he shifted with me, blocking my way, a long-fingered hand snaking around my waist to lean against the benchtop behind me.

"Not a lie. And no, I don't," I pressed a hand to Simon's chest, just hard enough to let him know my intent.

He looked down at my hand, amused. Simon snagged my waist, pulling me against him. "I'm not sure I can believe that," he murmured, and a thrill raced up my spine.

Lost for a moment in his stormy grey eyes, I could see how easily the tall, smooth-talking cowboy could become a lonely girl's infatuation. Him moving from ranch to ranch, leaving a trail of broken hearts in his wake.

The forbidden fruit.

But that wouldn't work here.

"I'm sure you can't," I grinned, tapping his chest again. "Love that shirt. Now, I need to—"

"Eve. Up for another round, honey?"

I peeked around the hard body in the crisp shirt in front of me. Archer leaned over the breakfast bar, twirling his half-empty glass between his hands. I looked down at the glass and back to him. He smiled, winking.

Get over here, he mouthed; *I'm saving your ass.*

I grinned, his eyes sparkling in return. Simon glanced over his shoulder, staring down at Archer, where he hunched over the benchtop. Taking the opportunity, I slid out from behind him as Archer downed the rest of his whiskey.

Grabbing Dad's best bottle and another tumbler, I poured myself a slim finger of the burnished liquid before I filled both glasses. Simon stood next to me the entire time, glaring at Archer, who seemed completely unaffected by the tall man. Not that Archer was short by any stretch of the imagination; he stood of a height with Jude who just topped six feet.

I capped the bottle, placing it in front of Archer.

"It's all yours," I murmured. "Tell Trav I said to share it with Jude and Dad. He won't be drinking much this year." I smiled through my sadness.

"You alright?" Archer asked under his breath.

"Thanks for the rescue." I looked up as Simon turned, stalking away from the kitchen with a pitcher of mulled wine and a handful of wine glasses protruding from his other hand. "Hang around any time, hey." I busied myself with cleanup, not daring to look at Archer again for fear of the rejection — or acceptance — I might see in his eyes.

His fingers tapped the counter, so close to my hand, I could feel the heat from his skin. I bit my lip, focusing on the already-clean benchtop I wiped.

By the time I'd finished my clean up, he'd returned to his place with the boys, calling insults at Travis, fitting right in.

The mulled wine sat on the table between them next to Dad's whiskey, but Simon had disappeared.

I debated going to find him but decided against it in the end. If I ran into him outside, there would be no Archer to rescue me. Even though I didn't *need* a rescuer, I had to admit that it had been an easier escape than I might have managed otherwise. Sometimes those exchanges could become nasty, and I hated how it put a pall on the whole evening.

I leaned over Trav's head, grabbing a glass, and slid comfortably between Jude and my brother, happy to fall in with their conversation for the night.

CHAPTER 5

"Grab his leg. No, that one," Jude instructed. The fawn kicked out, narrowly missing clipping Archer in the chin, but he moved just in time. "Good. Now that one."

I leaned over the enclosure's railing where we kept the young deer in with their mothers; this one had arrived out of season. Jude continued to instruct Archer on the finer points of hoof inspecting and clipping, though this little guy wouldn't need it for a while. Archer dealt with the animal competently, clearly glad he had a reason to stay around, though we would never send anyone away with the weather packing in as predicted.

Clouds gathered behind the mountain, sending a bitter wind down its steep sides. Seed heads and pine needles filled the air, while delicious scents flowed from the house. Mom had emerged, pottering around the big house, and with Simon's help, we'd managed to get Dad downstairs and comfortable.

Archer had taken off with Jude before breakfast, touring the fences closest to the house. We still needed to check the farthest ones. I slipped off the fence, looking between the stables. I wanted to go for a ride badly but taking Trav's truck would be faster. We'd have to hike to the far corner of the property where it boarded on Black Hill land, but otherwise, it was the fastest access.

"Hey. What are your plans for the afternoon?" Archer broke into my thoughts. I turned, smiling.

"I wanted to check the fences you guys didn't get to this morning before the weather hits us. Wanna go for a drive?"

Archer's eyes glinted. "Love to."

Jude helped me pack up everything I needed into the truck's bed while Archer grabbed food from the house. I'd planned well in advance, already having a basic lunch set out and water. Checking the fences would take most of the day.

"Are you alright to spare Archer?" I asked Jude, pausing with my hands on the rounds of wire.

Jude looked at me, his blue eyes piercing my meaning. "You're not comfortable with him." His head turned to the side. "You're *too* comfortable with him."

I flushed. "Would you guys stop doing that?" I grabbed my worn leather gloves. "Is he good to work with?"

"I think you can trust him, Eve. But if you want me to come with you..."

"I'll be fine. My phone's in the truck already, and I nicked Travis's charger, so you can reach me if I don't come back." I yawned. "Oh, too much mulled wine last night."

"It was a great batch," Jude agreed.

"Blame Simon. He did something to it. I need to find out what." I yawned again. "God, that's terrible. I need to wake up."

"He's an odd one."

"Who? Archer?" I asked, not thinking.

"Simon. Where's your head at, Eve?" He teased, nudging me. "Go on. You'll be fine. Call me if you need the extra hand. I serviced his truck last week; the filters are brand new."

He nodded to Archer approaching us with a bag slung over his shoulder and patted the side of the truck.

"Thanks," I said to Jude as he passed me the keys. Archer slung the bag into the passenger seat and climbed in after it.

I cranked the engine, which started easier than it had the last time I'd driven it and turned the truck around to head up along the ridge where the fence disappeared into the treeline. Jude held the gate open, shooing an inquisitive deer back. In the rear vision, he closed it behind us. I waved out the window, the tethers of the house and its occupants falling away as the truck trundled over the track through the field.

For some reason, Archer didn't count as an extra person in my bubble.

He fiddled with the music, searching through until he found Florida Georgia Line and turned it up.

I grinned at him, letting my shoulders drop back as music flowed over us.

"You've got good taste."

"Just working with what's already here." His gaze prickled my skin, my awareness of his presence heightening, though I didn't tense up.

The boundary line followed the ridge around to the mountain and passed the creek to the far corner. Granite blacks stood between the creek and the fence line, hence the hiking. I trundled the truck through the trees along the well-worn track.

Archer leaned back, taking in every inch of the property. "This is spectacular, Eve."

"That's one word for it." I smiled. Sharing the property with someone new never got old.

"It's nothing like—" Archer snorted softly, turning his head to look out the passenger window.

I hid a small grin. This man had a story, and I'd get it out of him, somehow.

"I thought we'd start along here, go out the back corner and follow the ridge as long as we can until we hit the creek. We're not missing any animals, so I don't expect any problems with the fence, but I want to check it, anyway."

"You really love the place."

"It's my home." The words were out of my mouth before I thought about them. Cringing, I looked at Archer. "I'm sorry, I didn't—"

"Eve. It's fine. You don't have to apologize for having a beautiful place on your doorstep. Thank you for wanting to share it with me."

I nodded, biting my lip.

"You're unusual, you know. The boys often fight me for the keys."

"You know where you're going. I've never been around here before."

"True," I conceded, "But usually the young cowboys want to show off, think they know the place better than I do."

"Hell. That's not going to happen with me." Archer snorted, grinning at me. "It must be painful."

"Oh, you have no idea," I replied, dropping the truck gently onto the track that followed the fence line.

"You might be surprised."

"Why's that?"

"Working with young cowboys is the same, anywhere," Archer said easily.

"Mmm." I shot him a glance, the forest thickening around us, casting long shadows over the cab of the truck. I looked a moment too late, his face shadowed in the darkness, and

I couldn't read his eyes. "Tell me about the last place you were at."

I let Archer regale me with tales of calves born in the middle of the night, chasing horses around small towns when gates were left open until we reached the creek. A small bridge wide enough to take the truck crossed it, but Trav and I had learned years ago the trail quickly turned to rocky outcrops unsuitable for horses or vehicles.

"Ready for a walk?" I checked my phone. Full battery, two bars of reception. Stuffing it into the back pocket of my jeans, I slipped out of the truck, leaving the keys in the ignition. Who would steal it out here?

Archer grabbed the bag of food, waving me off when I tried to take it from him and pocketed a few light tools so we wouldn't have to come all the way back to the truck if there were only small repairs — if any — to make.

Archer waited by the bridge. I led us deeper up the mountain, checking him when the trail disappeared to a few tape-marked trees.

"I can see why you'd never want to leave here."

"It sounds like you're in love with the place as much as I am."

"There aren't a lot of places you can truly be off the track these days.'"

"While still having phone reception. Well, sometimes, when you're out of the trees," I added, hauling myself over a large cube of granite, its speckled surface cool beneath my fingers. I planted myself on its edge, waiting for Archer to catch up.

"You're very blessed." Archer sat next to me, looking over the trees' tops to the fields before the house, the mountain its incredible backdrop as always. I smiled at his choice of words.

"You should see it in the spring. Wildflowers cover the fields, the deer in between. I can show you some promo shots we had done last season. Had a helicopter out here and all. But- it was just so beautiful. It would have been a waste not to save that."

"I'd love to."

I snuck a glance at him. Archer stared ahead, drinking it in.

"You're not going to be here to see it, are you?" I couldn't keep the flat edge from my voice.

He shook his head and turned to face me, his breath brushing my lips. My heart caught as his eyes found mine and dropped to my lips. "No, I won't. I'm not a stayer, Eve."

He drew a face full of regret back to hold mine for a long moment, then he climbed to his feet, holding out his hand.

I took it, letting his rough fingers curl around mine as he drew me up to him, so close his breath brushed my lips. I inhaled him — something earthy mixed with a touch of cinnamon and spice from the main house, and I knew I'd always associate this place with Christmas.

With him.

He squeezed my hand and stepped back, letting go. "Show me this back corner, huh?"

I swallowed and took him further up the ridge, leaving the bubbling brook and Red Hart behind us.

Cold sank to the forest floor, the chill reaching me even through my jacket. "God, it's going to be a cold night," I muttered, holding a low branch for Archer. He nodded, his gaze intense on me. I turned away, biting my lip. He hadn't spoken since we'd left the outcrop.

"Why did you leave the last place you were at? Not the *last* last, but the one place you loved?"

My back to him, I hoped it would give me a chance to get a real answer. I opened my mouth to say I wouldn't think less of him for not answering, but he beat me to it.

"My friend. Mentor. He was killed." The words came out softly. I stopped, my head whipping around.

"Oh, my god. I'm so sorry. I shouldn't have pried—"

"It's okay, Eve. I didn't have to answer."

"But you did." I held his dark gaze, staring deep into him. To my surprise, he dropped his guard and let me in.

"It broke me. For a time." Archer resumed walking. "Then I talked with some good friends, and they helped me to... find a path."

"Find a path? Are you the Dalai Lama now?" I teased lightly, not sure I understood.

"I went on a sort of hunt. Soul searching." Archer shrugged. I could see the term sat poorly with him.

"We do what we need to in times of grief. Tell me about your friend?"

Archer's shoulders tensed, and he shot me an indecipherable look. "You're... unique, Eve. He was, well, he was like my father. Maybe ten years younger. Taught me a lot about people and animals. We used to ride on our days off."

Where did you ride?

I wanted to ask, but I knew Archer wouldn't answer that one until he decided to tell me.

"You worked together and spent time off together? That's a pretty close friend."

"Family. He was my family."

I thought of Jude, working, and living with us for so many years. Travis' best friend.

"I understand."

Archer sent me another closed look. "Yes, I rather think you might."

We continued to walk in silence. Finally, the track met back up with the fence line, following it to the north corner. The top strand of wire barely twanged in my fingers, and by the time I'd made it another ten feet, it hung loosely through the top rail.

"That doesn't look right," Archer murmured behind me. Gritting my teeth, I shook my head.

"This," I waved to the adjoining land on the other side of the fence line, "is Black Hill land. If there's ever a problem on the ranch, it usually has to do with them."

"I understand," Archer tugged the wire gently. "That looks hellishly rocky over there." He nodded over the fence when I looked back at him.

"It is. They originally had some pasture land, but a few generations ago, a long-dead relative of theirs lost it in a card game."

"To you."

"To Red Hart," I agreed, reaching a place where the wire disappeared over a rock. We clambered over the small boulder, and I stared down in disbelief.

"What the—"

The next panels of the fence line to the corner where the line ended were dug up completely. The fence ended at the bottom of a cliff face, a long post wedged into a deep but narrow fissure, indicating where the land ended.

I counted the posts lying on their sides between the boulder and the cliff face, my brow furrowed as my mind turned over.

"Sixteen." Archer jumped down to the ground then turned with his arms raised. I slipped into them, letting him help me down without a thought, still staring. "Did you have livestock in this section?"

"A few bison," I replied, looking up at him. "I wondered why we hadn't seen any." I grabbed my phone out of my back pocket, firing off a message to Jude to get the remaining herd into the front pastures and close them off.

My phone beeped, but I didn't look at it, my attention held by movement closer to the cliff face.

"Pierce!" I yelled, striding along the uneven ground with sure steps. "What the hell have you—"

Pierce appeared between two trees, a swagger to his hips. Decorative boots that looked brand new paired against blue jeans and a starched shirt. With a white hat and silver lariat, he was the image of his father.

That wasn't a compliment.

Deep blue eyes that should have been attractive stared at me, his lips curling in a sneer. His face might be a handsome one, I supposed. All the lines and angles in the right places, but too much animosity between our families stole any remnant of beauty he might have for me.

"Eve. Glad you got to see the renovations. You see, a tree came down," Piece gestured behind him, but my eyes didn't leave his lying face, "and I had to work on this."

"How long, Pierce? You could have called me; you could have called Trav. You've got our numbers." I folded my arms over my chest, refusing to yell at him though I dearly wanted to. "How many Red Hart animals crossed over?"

"Oh, a few, I'm sure. We can sort the herds after Christmas."

"Are you kidding me? If we were friends, I'm sure that would happen, but we're not, Pierce. I don't trust an inch of you."

His eyes darkened. "Nor would I trust you." He muttered something under his breath, and my temper flared.

"What was that?"

Pierce opened his mouth with some remark, his eyes glittering, but Archer cut him off.

"Where's the tree?"

Pierce's brow creased. "What?"

I stifled a laugh, pressing my lips together as I caught what Archer had seen. Or, more to the point, not seen.

He stepped up behind me, sliding a hand familiarly onto my hip. His fingers slipped beneath my jacket, beneath the cotton of my shirt, the roughened tips pressing against my skin.

It took every inch of my control not to turn around and kiss him, but that would likely enrage Pierce further. His eyes dropped to my waist, his curled lips thinning to a pale strip of flesh.

I leaned back a little into Archer's warmth, glad for once of some support.

"The tree. That came down."

"Oh. We took it away." Pierce's smooth voice reminded me of Simon for a jarring moment, but I read the lie in his words.

"Bullshit. Where's the hole? Have you seen the age of these trees? A trunk like that would leave a hole where it came from, and nothing around is disturbed. You'll fix this, and you'll fix it this side of Christmas." I glared at my neighbor.

My phone beeped again in my pocket as Pierce opened his mouth. I held up a hand. "I don't want to hear it." I glanced at my phone, reading the message Jude had sent minutes ago, and clenched my teeth. "We have to go," I spoke to Archer and turned back to Pierce. "Fix this. NOW."

I turned away, heading back to the truck.

Archer's boots pounded the ground behind me. I kept the pace up until we hit the outcrop. Archer caught my arm, turning me to face him.

"What happened? I know you're angry, but—"

"Travis is hurt. One wall of the barn failed. I don't know. I need to get to him."

"Then, we go."

Grateful, I shot him a look and began to jog; some part of me pleased when he kept up.

Only a little breathless when we reached Trav's truck, I jerked when Archer's hand clamped over mine.

"You're worried. Let me, and let's get to your brother. I know where we're going."

I nodded, speechless, and sat in the passenger seat, clenching trembling hands. I read Jude's message, again and again, trying to eke more meaning from it, but the words were the same.

The south barn wall half-collapsed on your brother. He's okay. Sort of.

That *sort of* terrified me. If Trav had stopped breathing, Jude would still say he was sort of okay, just to calm me down.

I tapped my feet in an irregular rhythm; the noise irritated me. The truck trundled along the dirt track. I leaned over Archer's shoulder, surprised to see he took the truck along the path at a speed faster than I would have dared. I squeezed my hands together, a flush rising beneath my jacket. I shrugged out of it, squeezing that instead.

"What do you think the Black Hill boy used to pull out the fence posts?"

I threw my hands up. "I don't know. A donkey. A genie. I have no freaking idea."

"Too tight up there to bring a bulldozer in."

I smiled wanly. "Yeah, it is. No, I honestly have no idea, but thanks for the support."

He looked at me sideways for a quick moment then returned his attention to the road. "I wasn't sure if I might be overstepping... boundaries."

"Did you just make a fence line joke? Seriously?"

"Maybe."

I grinned. "You weren't overstepping at all. I really did appreciate you being there. I– Hell, I think I might actually have slapped him."

Archer sent me an amused look. "No."

"No?"

"No. You would have punched him. Hell, *I* wanted to punch him."

"See, this is why we get along."

The ranch came into view, and my jaw clamped shut with a snap that rattled my teeth. I clenched my jacket again, mumbling a *thanks* as Archer pulled up near the front of the house.

"Go. I'll park it and help Jude get the animals in."

CHAPTER 6

I sent prayers heavenward and shot out of my brother's truck, bursting through the double doors to the ranch house. Travis lay lengthwise across the sofa, a light blanket covering him. Simon settled on a pile of pillows on the floor next to my brother, holding up his phone. A video played on it.

"What happened? Are you okay?" I shot between Simon and Trav, pressing my hands over him. I lifted his shirt while he laughed at me. "There's no blood. Why aren't you in pain? I panicked my ass off for you!"

Simon pulled me off my twin. "Whoa, babe. Gentle with him. Got a broken leg, I think."

"You think? You *think?* Are you a doctor?" I twisted around in his hands.

Simon shook his head, his eyes narrowing as he looked at me. "No. I called the next best thing."

"Rachel." Travis shifted on the sofa, not wincing.

"You bothered Rachel with a broken leg? What's wrong with you two? She's a *vet!*" My voice rose several notches. I peered at Travis. "Why aren't you faint with pain? You're not superman. Are you drunk?"

"He's high."

My head spun on my neck so fast I could have been in a horror movie. I stared at Archer, where he stood, little more than a silhouette in the doorway.

"What?"

"I suspect your new friend here has dosed him with an opiate. It's removed the connection to his pain receptors — for now. Are you having anyone fly in?"

I blinked at Archer's businesslike tone. Simon stood.

"Why? Do you have a doctor on speed dial?" His aggressive tone shook me.

I frowned, but I knew people did odd things in times of heightened emotion. Hell, I'd just busted in, demanding answers. But Trav was my brother. More than that, he was my twin. I had to have some rights for that, but maybe I *had* been too aggressive.

"I think you've done enough, perhaps?" I let my words hang, my eyes telling him where he sat in the pecking order of my family. Simon huffed and stayed silent on his spot on the floor.

Archer raised an eyebrow. I suppressed a giggle, slapping my hand over my mouth, though a squeak escaped. Archer rolled his eyes at me. I giggled harder.

"Okay, now we've ascertained your brother is not in mortal danger, can I have a few hands to help me collect the herd? Damn things are spread over the entire property."

People I didn't know were in the house moved at Archer's call to action. I rose, but he stepped forward through the small throng as they filtered out the door and stopped me.

"Not you, Eve."

I pressed my lips together for a second and saw his own twitch.

"What?"

"Honey, I can tell when you're preparing to rip me a new one by now. But it's not the right time." His tone gentled. "Stay with your brother. Make sure whatever he's had doesn't..."

"Overdose him." I shot a look back at Travis. Simon settled back on his pillows. "Oh, hell. Will you—"

"I'll take Haldon with me." Simon perked up at his name, eyeing me with interest. "Jude has the animals in hand. We'll get it done. Look after your family." His head dipped, and for a tiny second, I thought he might kiss me.

Archer straightened with a soft sigh I knew was only meant for me to hear. My lips tingled with the urge to brush them over the few days' growth on his chin.

"I will." I whispered, "Thank you."

That earned me a quick grin. "We'll be back tonight."

"I want to help," I protested.

"You are. Please, look after him." Archer frowned. "Where's my favorite songstress?"

I blinked, looking for Mom. Guilt swamped me. I looked around. The house seemed empty, apart from Travis and us, playing with Simon's phone.

"I didn't even—"

"It's okay, Eve." He raised a hand and dropped it again.

I gave him a weak grin. "How many times are you going to say that?"

"As many as it takes for you to believe it." He dipped his head, hesitating, but this time he brushed his lips over my cheek, the corner of his lips touching mine. My eyes drifted shut, encompassed in the musky, spicy scent of him, and when I opened them again, Archer was gone.

I looked for Mom and found her in my bed, completely passed out. I tucked her in, reasoning that I didn't need my own bed for the night, and left her there, liberating the teacup on my bed stand.

Swishing the remains of the tea in the cup, I stared into the tea leaves, wishing I could read them. With Black Hill attacking from one side, Dad and Travis down, concern quickly ran to fear for the future of the ranch.

I drained the rest of them as I walked down the stairs, placing the cup in the kitchen. Exhaustion slapped me the moment I stopped. The staff would have to fend for themselves for one night. Thank God I had Jude, though Archer was certainly handy, and even Simon. He might have doped my brother up, but he'd had good intentions.

I sank onto the pillows Simon had previously occupied, leaning my head on Travis' stomach. He snored softly, bringing up all the years as kids we'd fought our sleep and climbed first into each other's cots, then beds as we grew. Not out of any taboo desire but simply to be close to the womb buddy we'd been created near.

If something happened to him — tears I hadn't known I'd held back, began to flow. The stress of the day weighing on me, salt ran down my cheeks, and I let my eyes fall shut.

Voices intruded on my rest, hands slipping around my chest. I shifted against my pillow, comfortable.

"Come on, honey. You can't sleep here." I mewled at Archer's voice, stretching. His hands squeezed my ribs.

"Don't move her. She's fine."

Was that Simon? I squinted, bright light assailing my eyes, and shut them tight again.

"Come on, Eve."

Archer. Sweet Archer. After this afternoon, I knew I'd do anything he asked — albeit grumpily.

"It's bright," I protested.

"I'll get the light." His hands left me for a moment, and I sank back into sleep. The next time I opened my eyes, darkness covered the still house.

"Archer?" I whispered, trying to find him, but the pitch black before my eyes refused to dissipate.

"I got you, honey." His hands shifted. I moved, inhaling him. My cheek pressed to the cotton of his shirt, his arm wrapped around me. I knew I should flinch, be surprised, or pull away, especially after the issue I'd taken with Simon, but Archer made a great pillow. Combined with my crash and burn of earlier, I couldn't bring myself to move.

"Why are we sitting in the dark?"

"You refused to leave your brother after Rachel came to check him, and we can't move him tonight. I couldn't leave you on the floor, and with your bed already occupied, I thought I might keep you company."

"Oh." I yawned, pressing a hand to my head. "Ouch. I don't remember Rachel being here."

"You were pretty out of it." His chest moved beneath me. I blinked in the darkness, sorting where my limbs were over his body to find myself draped across him.

"This isn't a good idea," I mumbled into his chest, making a half-hearted attempt to move, but even I had to admit it was a pretty poor protest.

His arm pressed around my waist. "Stay there. It's only an hour 'til dawn, and you're comfortable."

"I am?"

"Yes." His chest moved again. I raised my head to peer at him suspiciously in the darkness.

"Are you laughing at me?"

"Only a little."

His hand stroked the length of my back in a steady motion.

"Oh. Is Trav okay?"

"He is for now. Sleep, Eve. You're going to need it."

I was? Letting him press my head back to his chest, I sank into the warmth and comfort he offered, my eyes drifting shut.

Archer's hand stroked along my back, taking me deeper into sleep. I struggled against it to stay awake, my mind beginning to click over.

"Why can't I remember Rachel being here?" I asked, frowning. I pressed up, but he pulled me gently back. "She's my friend; I would have wanted to speak to her. I *do* want to speak to her. Archer?" I prompted when he didn't answer.

He sighed, his hand drifting up to my hair. His fingers tangled lightly into the long strands that formed a curtain that flowed over both my shoulders and back, massaging into my scalp. I moaned softly, and his chest rumbled in response.

"Did you have anything to drink when we got back? I know you haven't eaten dinner..."

I shook my head in a small movement, not wanting to dislodge his hand as his fingers drew pleasure along my spine. "No. I don't think so. Oh, I finished Mom's teacup."

Archer stayed silent this time, no matter how I prodded him. His massage slid down my neck, his fingers working firm circles into tight muscles there. "You carry your stress here."

"And my lower back," I said softly.

"Do you want me to do that too?"

I paused, my hand pressed against the hard ridges of muscle beneath his shirt. Did I? His touch soothed tense muscles. Though I desperately wanted him to continue, saying so felt too much like an invitation. "Not right now," I murmured from where I lay half across him.

So much for no invitations.

I mentally rolled my eyes at myself. Apparently, my mushy head also lowered my inhibitions. I tried to concentrate on what Archer said, but my eyes grew blurry, and I closed them for a minute more, listening to the comforting thud of his heart.

Outside, the sky grew lighter with the false dawn, movement beginning outside. From my place half propped against Archer's chest, I watched a shadow I recognized as Jude's cross the yard, heading into the barn.

"We need to fix that wall in the barn," I yawned, covering my mouth. "My God, I'm tired. What's happening with Trav? Will he need to go somewhere?"

"He probably does," Archer shifted beneath me, stretching. "But if he does, well. That's another thing. Who's your closest doctor?"

"You met her last night." I sat up, pushing my hair off my face. "I'll call into town. He might have to be flown to a hospital. God, he'll hate being off the ranch." I straightened, rolling my shoulders, and opened my eyes fully.

Archer sat only a few inches away, his eyes full of shadows. I paused, staring at him. His hand rose slowly, catching loose hairs that had escaped my brief tidy up. He wound them around his fingers, tugging a little as his gaze dropped to my lips.

My breath caught as he tucked the hair behind my ear, his knuckles grazing my cheek. He stopped for a moment then pushed away, rising.

"I'd better help Jude. Get some rest, Eve."

I leaned back against Travis' good leg, watching as Archer descended the few steps to the yard, crossing it with long strides, his touch still burning my cheek.

I stared at the barn doors. Jude and Archer hung off one each, ladders beneath their feet working hard to keep the men in one place as they both clambered across the front of the barn. A deep red with white struts and cross beams, the thing had stood forever, with minor — okay, major — adjustments. Dad had maintained it, passing the torch to Jude and Travis when they were in their early twenties and teaching them everything they knew.

But looking at it, walking around the underside of the great pair of sliding doors, *nothing* told me it would fail.

No rust, nothing big or bent that would make it fail.

Nothing.

I walked backwards from the huge pair of double doors, studying them. My brother had been airlifted to the county hospital earlier this morning, which meant he would be spending Christmas alone, though I suspected Rachel would keep him company.

Mom had gone back up to sit with Dad afterward, her thin shoulders warped beneath the weight of an injured son she couldn't be with and a husband she could do little for. I'd promised tea, but by the time I'd brought it up, she'd fallen asleep again, her bony hand wrapped around his.

I worried for them both, and Trav. Losing my twin's company, his support in such a stressful time, made my steps heavier. I had a good idea of how Mom must feel and envied her ability to sleep through it.

Unfortunately, I had to adult.

The boys had let me watch their investigation into what had happened to the doors but wanted me to stay away. I remained at a safe distance, though I wanted to be part of the investigation that helped work out what had happened to my brother.

More reports of the weather closing in found us daily, predicting not just the picturesque white Christmas that glammed Red Hart up each year but a complete whiteout. Trav had gotten away safely; I still expected him to bitch his way through the season until he could return. The paramedics had assured me they would pass on our details and keep us up to date on all things Travis.

I'd wondered if Jude would be lonely without him, but he appeared to have found a kindred spirit in Archer. The two were getting along famously. Part of me knew Travis would have cast his pall of jealousy over the proceedings if he were still here to see it.

Simon and some of the younger hands headed to the North-Eastern corner to fix the mess Pierce had made of the fence line. I prayed his father Bill wouldn't make an appearance, a crotchety man who argued over everything in front of him — even if he stood on the losing side.

"This one's good," Jude called, sliding down his ladder with his feet to the sides, work-earned muscles rippling beneath his shirt. Thankfully, he wore leather gloves. His well-muscled shoulder blades jutted from beneath his shirt, and I thought again that this man needed a woman. Then I remembered my promise to myself and quickly let it go.

Jude's boots hit the ground with a puff of dust.

"This one's not." Archer curved around the door frame, hanging slightly upside down from it. The door that had fallen on my brother now leaned against the barn. I watched Archer contort himself in discovery mode. "Here. It's been scratched to shit." He tossed a tool to the ground, where it promptly sank into an excess of straw. A part of it glinted in the morning sun, and I memorized the spot.

"Show me."

Ignoring Jude's protests, I walked beneath where Archer worked.

"See? Here." He pointed with a leather-gloved finger I didn't recognize as one of our ranch sets, available for anyone to use.

Only a good cowboy brings his own gloves.

I remembered Mama saying it years ago when she taught me how to judge whether a cowboy might be a good worker and had taken stock then, my chest expanding at the thought of finding such a man one day while I watched Dad work the tractor. As I looked up at Archer, that same feeling cleared my lungs, and I breathed deeply, inhaling leather, animals, and last night's whiskey.

"Ahh, Eve?" I looked up at Archer's tone. "You might want to move there, honey."

"Oh. Sorry." I stepped back, still watching, then turned, heading away as the younger guys began to refit the door. Bent but reformed, the thing was in no condition to be rehung. Either Archer or Jude could roast them for it later, and I was happy to pass the buck on that.

"It's fine, honey."

I nodded to his comment, a sparkle in the straw catching my eye. I bent to retrieve it, a thin sleeve of metal pressed together at one end to form a pin.

"No, no, get that the fu– get that out of here!" Jude yelled, apologizing to me with a wave.

I nodded, still staring at the pin, turning it over in my hand. The bottom bore scratches where something had scraped its surface in a pushing motion, had it held the door together. I turned back to Jude and Archer, waving the metal clip over my head.

"Is this what you're looking for?"

Jude looked down at me with a frown, pausing as he berated the remaining hands and waved them away. Archer gripped the top of the door frame, hanging for a moment, and dropped to the ground.

Jude reached me first. I tipped the metal sleeve into his gloved hand and let him turn it over, leaving him to work out what had happened while I examined the door myself. The hands were gathered in a cluster of clean shirts. A wolf whistle came from somewhere deep in the huddle, and I knew they'd never oust the one responsible — safety in numbers and all. I waved them over to the deer with instructions to separate the harts from the mothers with a wry grin.

I couldn't deal with an unexpected pregnancy at this point in the season since Archer and the boys had put all my livestock into one place last night. A dull headache thumped behind my eyes. I pressed my hand to my forehead, wishing I'd done something to earn my hangover apart from sleeping on Archer's chest.

Rotating my neck, I studied the door frame without the interference of the farmhands. A dent poked out where it had collided with my brother, an L-shape evident where his knee, or maybe his hip, had made contact with the metal.

Climbing half up onto the door, I looked at how the roller worked. A bolt that held the roller in place, but what held the door up? I peered beneath, not really having had to study the thing before, and found a small, dual hole.

"This." Archer's voice sent a shiver along my shoulder I fought hard to conceal as he stood behind me, holding out the pin I'd given

Jude into my peripheral vision. "It's been removed or forced out. Same scratches above."

He swiped his hair over his head, the dangling locked pushed away from his face.

"Yes, I suppose it was," I said neutrally.

His eyes narrowed as Jude joined him. "What is it?" His voice had a sharp tone I instantly hated, feeling like a butterfly pinned under a microscope, fighting to prove my worth.

I took a deep breath and gave in.

"You and Mr. Haldon arrive on the same day, and since then, we've had nothing but trouble," I snapped. "My brother isn't here, my father is laid up in bed with my mother in a flurry, the fence line at the northeast corner is a fucking mess, and this happens to my brother. I mean, what else can happen?"

Archer held his silence for a moment, assessing me with that steady gaze. "And you've got Black Hill boy," he mused, his eyes settling on me, ignoring my outburst. "He seems to cause regular trouble."

A cold wind whipped the nape of my neck, sending a shiver along my shoulders that had nothing to do with the two men before me.

"Len's turn wasn't anyone's fault, Eve," Jude murmured softly as Archer spoke up at the same time.

"You don't need to bear this alone."

"Isn't it?" I snapped at Jude. "Maybe if I'd gotten my ass off my computer and done a bit more, Dad wouldn't have had a stroke. And you," I wheeled on Archer, "you just got here, so don't you dare." I waved a finger at him, unable to finish my threat. Archer watched me while Jude kicked at the dirt, muttering.

I couldn't stand to be near either of them, or myself.

Stalking through the barn to the stalls where I saddled my favorite mare, Gigi, and took her out the south end of the barn at a canter with no warm up.

128

CHAPTER 7

The wind brushed my cheeks as I rode away from the barn, heading into the tree line. A path ran up the hillside there, ending in a natural copse of trees with a small clearing in the center.

I'd wanted to ride, but my plan to get away from everything hadn't included going off at the people who supported me to do it. As Gigi's hoofs pounded the ground, the knot in my chest loosened with her steady rhythm. Neither of the men had earned my words, though they'd bore the brunt of them.

I'd run away like a child having a tantrum. I shook my hair out as my mare slowed to a steady trot once we were well inside the treeline. Shadows covered the pine mulch that carpeted the forest floor, releasing a mixture of both sharp and sweet scents, the earth beneath leaving a lasting impression.

My shoulders dropped back. I rolled them, knowing I had to go back to apologize to both Jude and Archer. But not right away. For now, I needed to be away from everyone for a while longer.

The trees tightened into the wall of trunks, the lowest branches well above my head. The path led between them, disappearing into the dim light that filtered from the canopy above. With the closeness of the trees, the air here warmed, the spruce all the more potent, as though I were doused in Christmas.

The mare wound her way between the trunks. I had to admit that if I didn't know the area, the forest's dark section would be daunting.

But to me, it was magical.

My anger and frustration dithered at the edges of my conscience, but they had no power here. Stress I hadn't known I was carrying rolled away from my shoulders. I inhaled deeply through my nose, smiling as memories bombarded me.

Gigi snickered as she wandered between two thick trunks. On the other side, it opened out into a circular clearing, almost like a fairy ring.

I laughed, remembering Travis chasing me after I'd persuaded him to wear glitter wings, zooming around the clearing while I berated him for not fluttering the right way.

My horse stopped. I slipped off her back, my boots hitting the soft, springy ground. Moss grew in patches, pine needles piling around it, a burst of color in the earth tones. Gigi wandered off to a patch of grass that looked like it had grown there simply for the purpose of feeding her.

The clearing had a peace, a serenity, lying deep in the forest — it always had been, and growing up, nothing had changed about this place. It did me good to clear my own mind, to have a mini reset before I went back.

Closing my eyes, I stood in the very center, letting my arms hang loosely by my sides. My head tipped back, shadows and light dancing on the inside of my eyelids. I breathed in, letting the seasonal scents bathe me in the heaviness of the forest. Swaying, I got drunk on the serenity of the place, on memories of a brother I loved so much, but now I wouldn't be spending Christmas with.

It seemed like such a small, insignificant thing, but it mattered to my heart, and I couldn't — *I wouldn't* — change that.

The stresses of this season swirled around my head. Dad laid up, and Mom no better, though I didn't blame her; her exhaustion was all too understandable. With Travis gone and Pierce being his usual charmingly assholic self, accidents around the ranch... I gritted my teeth as the enormity of the job stretching into the future hit the boiling point.

A scream bubbled in my throat, longing to be voiced. I breathed deeply. I had Jude. Thank the Lord, I had Jude. Without him, the ranch would be in poor condition. I had Archer, and Simon provided some help. Plus, the younger hands, who were generally well behaved. And me.

I could do this.

We could do this.

Opening my eyes, the weight of my stress, the darkness of my anger and blame fell away. I shook my shoulders, able to stand under my own weight without being encumbered by the mess of emotions that had roiled over me.

Gigi still munched at her clump of grass. I let her trim it down to an even length all over, collecting her reins in one hand.

My desire to ride diminished, I walked with her back through the forest. We circled behind the house by rote memory rather than by design; the path Travis and I had always taken to extend our playtime when Mom called us in.

I studied the house, somewhat darker this year. The life seemed gone from it. I hoped no one who saw it, but doubt crept over me. With Dad well out of commission and Travis in the hospital, I needed to lift the house up for the next few days or weeks until we could create a new normal with the rise of the new year.

A small building rose between the trees. I blinked in surprise at Archer's cabin, realizing how long I'd been lost in my thoughts. I grinned, patting Gigi's side. She whickered softly and pulled at my hand. I let her head to the water trough attached to the side of the cabin.

"It's empty, you goose. See? There's nothing to drink—" I closed my mouth as she stretched her long neck to the half-full trough, lapping at the water with enthusiasm.

A footstep crunched the leaf mulch behind me. I hid a smile.

"Did you do this? She's very appreciative."

I turned on my heel to face Archer. He raised an eyebrow, rocking back on his heels.

"Yes, she is, and no, I didn't."

"You didn't?" I frowned. "Do we have a leak, then?" I ran my hands over the pipes that connected the guttering and tank to the trough, but nothing was unusual.

"Pretty specific leak." Archer followed me, watching from a few feet away. "Eve..."

I straightened, narrowly missing banging my head on the edge of the trough. "You're right; I'm sorry. Neither of you deserved to be on the other end of my fears. Though I'm sure Jude and I have a tally system," I mused, still watching my horse. I felt Archer's eyes on my back and turned. "Sorry, that was a terrible apology."

He held up a hand. "It's fine. You're under a hell of a lot of pressure with family and illnesses — your brother messaged. The vet is staying with him."

"Rachel is? Oh, my god. He's got no sense. She needs to spend time with her own family. It's Christmas, for fuck's sake," I grumbled, folding my arms. Archer gripped my shoulders and turned me to face him fully.

"He's in the hospital with no one to look after him for now. The distance doesn't matter, Eve. He's away, and she obviously needs him."

"When did you become a relationship coach?" I needled, but my heart wasn't in the argument. "You're right, of course."

I ran my hands over my hair, feeling the cooler edge to the wind that blew up the foot of the mountain from this angle.

"I know how people work." Archer gathered Gigi's reins, looping them over a post that had been out of use for many years. "Come on. You look like you could use a coffee without Jude and... anyone else badgering you."

I smiled back. "Please. That would be lovely." I followed him to the door, the wind blasting my back with an icy edge despite the sun. "When that tail turns warm, you know the snow's on the way," I muttered, kicking my boots into a pile by the door.

Warmth drew me into the cabin. I shrugged my jacket off, hanging it next to his on the rack by the door, feeling stupidly domestic.

"Milk's in the fridge." Archer nudged me out of the doorway, closing it behind us. He drew a jar of instant down while I searched the cupboards for mugs.

"I thought I knew where things were," I kept searching. Archer passed me two mugs with a grin.

"I might have moved some things about." A warm mug filled with coffee found its way into my hands. I breathed it in.

"Thank you."

"They're your supplies."

"But, it's your space."

"You're in an argumentative mood today, huh?"

I considered. I had been, earlier. But the walk back around the and my time in the forest had done me good, stripped me back to a reset. More time in my head, but I didn't need to sound crazier than I already did today.

"Nah, I'm good now." I sipped my coffee.

Archer raised an eyebrow over the lip of his own steaming mug, the hint of a smile curling his lips. "If you say so."

"I do." I sipped my coffee again, then sniffed the steam above it. "What did you do to this? It's delicious! Wait, is that..."

"Cinnamon and ginger." Archer smiled fully, this time. "Haldon isn't the only one who can cook."

"So I can see."

I looked at him, really looked at him for the first time. The firm line of his shoulders, straight beneath his cotton shirt, which bore some grime but was not really worn around the edges. At least not the way some of the cowboys' who came through dressed.

The cuffs were dirty, some dust across his chest, but all that could be from a day's — or morning's — work. No, this shirt was new. My gaze traveled over well-muscled thighs that filled his jeans, a firm fit but not tight; darkened at the knees and cuffs from work, but the same as his shirt, there were no thin patches, threadbare sections.

His worn belt buckle where it looked like he'd rubbed it with his thumbs, perhaps, and crinkles on his leather belt the only older items on him, though I knew his boots had some scuffing. Still, they were an expensive cut.

"What do you see, Eve?" His eyes held a question, with no fear behind it. They still sparkled, keeping his identity locked away behind the sharp mind that guarded his secrets.

I had an inkling that I only had to ask, and he'd tell me, but it wasn't in me to pry. If he wanted to keep his secrets, I'd accept that — providing they didn't negatively impact the workings of the ranch.

I shook my head. "I see a hard-working man trying to fit in." I sipped my coffee again and found I'd almost finished it. "Maybe trying to find yourself," I murmured, finishing the cup.

Archer's fingers closed around mine, removing the mug from my grip. He placed it on the coffee table, not releasing my hand.

Butterflies rioted deep in my stomach. I didn't dare move as he turned back to me, his fingers warm from handling the mugs brushing my cheek. He tucked strands of hair behind my ear, curling them around his finger. My lips parted, but no breath escaped; I wasn't sure I had breath left to share.

Archer leaned forward, his gaze flicking between my eyes and my mouth. His hand slid beneath my hair, cupping the back of my head, and I leaned into his touch, letting go of a soft breath.

It was as if he'd been waiting for the response. His arms wound around me as he drew me along the couch to him, his mouth pressing down over mine. The leather-earthy scent of him overwhelmed me, sending my head swimming as my eyes flickered closed.

My hands wrapped around his upper arms, discovering solid muscle there, I knew only came from years of hard, manual labor. For some reason, somewhere in the depths of my mind, that made him hellishly sexy.

His tongue swept across my lips, and I opened them with a gasp, bolts of desire shooting through me. He explored me, tasting, stroking until I melted like butter in his arms.

He groaned in response, pulling me harder against his chest, tugging on my hair to tip my head back. I arched against him, my hands crumpling the cotton of his shirt.

Cinnamon and gingerbread surrounded me, pulling me deeper into him. I drew back a little, and he stopped, his eyes holding a new question.

"It's okay," I whispered, reassuring him, trying to slow my breath, but my chest still rose too fast, "I just wanted to—" I unclenched my hands from his shirt, brushing them over the stubble on his chin. It wasn't as long as I had thought, the sharp ends pricking my fingertips.

I smiled, wondering how it would feel against sensitive skin elsewhere, and made the mistake of looking up into his eyes. He read my thoughts in an instant, his hands curving around my hips. Lifting me, his hands curled beneath my legs to straddle him. I gasped as he pressed me down onto him, his hands tangling in my hair to draw my mouth back to his.

"Eve," he growled softly, his lips brushing back and forth across mine, "we have to get up."

"Why?" I whispered back, responding to every kiss, every touch with one of my own. He plucked my shirt out from my jeans, roughened hands sliding up my back, his kisses harder, more insistent.

"Because if we don't, I'm going to fuck you right here."

"Oh," I said softly, pressing against his chest, licking his bottom lip, not particularly adverse to that idea.

His hands flexed on my back.

"Eve?"

"Mm?"

"Honey, I need you to—" he broke off as my fingers found the top button of his shirt, fiddling with it.

His hand closed around mine, squeezing gently. The squeeze became a caress, his thumb rubbing over the sensitive skin inside my wrist. I moaned softly, his every touch leaving a searing impression, a brand on my skin I hoped would never fade.

"Stay," I murmured, still fiddling with the button. "Stay with me." His hands flexed in my hair, and he kissed me hard, breaking away with a groan of his own.

"What?"

"Don't go home." I closed my eyes as soon as the words were out of my mouth. "Disregard. That's lack of sleep, and possibly hormones talking. Stay and go as you need. It's got nothing to do with me."

"It's got everything to do with you," Archer rasped, releasing my hand to wrap his around my waist.

His lips pressed gently against mine, then not so gently. Squeezing my skin, his fingers slid under the edge of my jeans, seeking the softer flesh beneath. His mouth pressed harder against mine, nipping in tiny, soft bites, pressing kisses over the top.

I leaned into him, running my hands over his shirt. He laughed against my mouth, tangling his hand in my hair, drawing my head back to press a trail of kisses along my throat to my collarbone and back up again.

I whimpered, drawing his mouth back to mine. My hands went on a tour of their own, curving my fingers over the ridges of muscle I'd seen before, discovering the hardened man beneath his clothes. I shifted, needing to be closer to him, to press my skin against his.

His tongue stroked over mine, drawing moans from my throat. The stubble of his beard scratched my chin as I drew back, gasping for air, but he pulled my head down, refusing to let me break the kiss again. His hands returned to my waist, squeezing, drawing me against him.

Archer pressed down hard on my hip. I cried out, my eyes flying open at the pressure of the hardness of him against me through the thin barrier of my jeans. He rocked me gently against him, his fingers sliding around to the front of my jeans, playing with the button there. I bit back a moan, nodding.

Eyes hooded, he kissed me again, no question in them, no resistance there this time. His hand wound around the back of my neck, pulling me down to him.

"Eve," he whispered, drawing back.

A knock broke my concentration. After a long moment, I realized the sound came from the door. I froze, my hands curling around his, suddenly unsure. It had been a long time since I'd been intimate with anyone. I wasn't sure I was ready to share this with another person intruding on my precious moment.

"Should I—" I blinked, his fingers tracing the curve of my cheek, closing around my neck in a gentle but incredible arousing movement. His thumb stroked the join of my neck and shoulder, and he made no move to answer the door.

"It's not locked," Archer murmured, his hands finding my hips again, squeezing tight.

I whimpered softly, letting him draw my mouth back to his. Archer kissed me languidly; deep, slow kisses that sent my head whirling. I closed my eyes and fell into him.

The door flew open. I blinked lazily, turning my head just enough to see the blurry figure in the doorway of Archer's cabin. I squeezed my eyes shut again, then opened them. Simon's face came into focus, his mouth agape as I leaned into Archer.

I made to wriggle off him, but the warm hands on my hips held firm.

"What do you want, Haldon?" Archer asked softly, tracing the curves of my ass with his fingertips, down the outside of my thighs and back up again.

I shivered under his touch, squeezing his shoulders. "Archer," I whispered, turning back to him as he drew me closer.

Simon's gaze burned into my back. I clung to Archer's shoulders, wishing he would leave.

"Eve," Simon said my name as though he hadn't interrupted us, "your mother needs you. At the house."

I glanced over my shoulder, locking eyes with the other man. His lip curled into a sneer as he stared at me. I shivered, Archer's arms wrapping tight around me, forming a partial barrier between us. Simon's eyes burning a trail over the both of us, he stepped back, half closing the door. His shadow moved away from the doorway, but some part of me knew he hadn't left yet.

Archer's fingers caught my chin, turning me back to him. He held my gaze for a long moment, unspeaking. His eyes darkened at whatever he saw there, his gaze dropping to my lips. The only hint of his intention before he rolled me, pinning me beneath him on the sofa, and kissed the hell out of me.

I gasped, writhing beneath him as he slid his legs between mine, every inch of him pressed firmly against me.

"Fuck, Eve," Archer groaned, a thrill racing through me at the way he said my name. "Damn." He raised up on his forearms, braced over me.

"Please," I whispered, hating the begging tone in my voice.

"If you say that again, I won't get up without fucking you."

My lips parted to — *argue, say it again* — when his mouth slammed down against mine. His kisses came hard, rough, raising desires I didn't know I had. His tongue ravished my mouth, not stopping. This was no gentle, sweet kiss; this was a hell of a prelude to sex. I arched beneath him, his groans answering my whimpers.

"We have to get up," he rasped against my lips, tracing the shape of them with his tongue. My hips writhed, finding the perfect fit against him. He moaned softly into my mouth, pressing himself into me until I gasped.

His mouth tore from mine, his hands finding my wrists as he broke the kiss, hauling me upright.

"Are you kidding? What the hell was that?"

He scraped a hand over his head. "Me taking advantage of a woman who should be with her family," he said firmly, sitting back and drawing me up against him. My gaze darted to the door, still ajar, but the shadows behind it were empty.

"No. That was whatever has been building up between us."

Archer's dark gaze settled on me, intense and assessing. "Which was?"

My temper flared. "Was it just lust, Archer? Tell me, what did you feel?"

"Perhaps it's just a lonely woman and a man with too much pent-up energy."

"Are you trying to be an asshole? Because it's working," I snapped back, my hands still twined in his.

Archer's thumb brushed across my inner wrist again. I sighed, my body responding the same way as it had before. His nostrils flared, a sharp breath hitting my lips. I leaned into him, but he wound his hand in my hair, holding me away. My eyes snapped wide.

"You need to get back to the house. See what your mother needs."

"That doesn't change this," I countered.

"Doesn't it?" He raised an eyebrow, and I wanted to slap it away. "Go back to your family, Eve. Help them."

"Simon knows. There are never any secrets on the ranch. Everyone knows everything." I paused, reading some extra knowledge in

Archer's eyes I wasn't privy to, but he wasn't forthcoming. "He made a pass at me. In the kitchen."

"Did he?" Archer's voice was flat.

"Yes."

Do you care?

"You should get back to your family," Archer repeated, squeezing my fingers as I opened my mouth to argue, hauling me off the sofa.

I took the time to straighten my hair before we left the cabin.

Archer waited for me outside. I circled the cabin, blinking at the ground.

"Eve? Honey, what are you doing?"

"I've lost my horse," I muttered, crouching to study the ground, but it was too messed with our own footprints.

"Haldon took it. Her."

I stared at him, incredulous. "Why would he do that? How do you know?"

Archer pointed to the path leading back to the big house. Shod hoof prints were clearly outlined there. I gritted my teeth, trying to straighten my hair. Archer watched me.

"Reckon he did it as a reason to be up here. You ready to go back?"

I swallowed. Was I?

"Yeah." I straightened, tugging at my shirt, but the material bore the lines of our make-out session.

Archer's fingers brushed my chin. I looked up at him, my heart thundering.

Too close. You're too close.

"You look beautiful," he murmured, brushing his knuckles over my cheek. My heartbeat settled, inhaling long, even breaths.

I nodded, matching his stride back to the ranch house.

CHAPTER 8

Simon and Jude were bent in conversation when Archer and I approached the verandah. He hadn't said a word the entire way, reaching out to squeeze my hand only once in the walk back to the house.

Torn somewhere between frustrated and heartache, I could only blame myself for breaking my own set of house rules. But the one time I gave in to any feelings I might have, I had to admit the rejection stung.

My fingers twitched, itching to brush his hand, to feel them wind through my hair. I inhaled sharply, stepping up onto the verandah. Just as I thought I'd managed to pull myself together, Archer's hand pressed against my lower back, steadying me, though I didn't need it.

My eyes opened wide, the toe of my boot catching on the top step, and I stumbled. Archer's hands wound around me, setting me straight.

Wish granted.

I silently cursed myself, grinning at Jude to cover my shock. Simon's hard eyes stared into mine, the same cold shiver as before working its way along my spine.

I shifted backward a half step, frowning at his hostility.

Just because I turned him down.

Archer offered a hand, and I gripped it, more in need of moral support than anything else at that moment. I winced, realizing I could be in the same boat with him as Simon appeared to be with me.

"Girl's never been able to stay on her feet." Jude grinned.

I strode across the verandah, glaring at him in faux rage. "That's not true!"

I whacked his arm for good measure. Jude mouthed "*ow,*" rubbing his arm. My hand stung, and I rubbed it on my jeans. Jude's head swung back to Simon, and Archer stepped in front of me, his hand out.

"What did you say?" Jude looked perplexed, but the little I could see of Archer's face was dark and closed.

Simon laughed, an unconvincing sound on the silent porch.

"Just said she doesn't need to stay on her feet if she's on her back." He laughed again, collecting his hat and slipping it on. "Guess I'll be working, then."

I blinked, disregarding the heat in my cheeks, and turned back to Jude, searching for something to break the moment.

"Sorry, I didn't mean to hit you so hard. And I'm sorry about before."

Both men stared at me. Jude cleared his throat.

"It's all good. You hit like a girl." He winked at me. I smiled back, relieved of his good humor. He sneaked a quick look at Archer. "Ah– a few deer are missing. The mother and fawn. A few bison. I sent a crew out to find them. Told them not to cross into Black Hill land. Doubt they'll listen." He sent me a look full of meaning. I walked off the edge of the verandah to look at the sky, turning in a circle.

"Well, fuck," I swore. "Where did Trav leave my keys?"

"He took them with him," Jude apologized, his hands up as I stalked towards him.

"He *what?*"

"It was an accident. He had them in his pocket the whole time. I know." He patted my shoulder in commiseration as I continued to swear. "Here's his keys. No, stop cussing. You're meant to be a woman."

That earned him a second slap, but with substantially less force than the first one.

"Where have you looked?" Archer jumped in, shrugging into his coat he'd left on the coat rack outside the double doors.

"Everywhere." Jude ran a hand over his short hair. Even unshaven and a touch disorderly, he was still a classic cowboy, the evening shadow only enhancing his good looks.

Dark circles hung under his eyes, and I realized with a start how little rest *he* must have had in the last two days. Plus, his best friend currently occupied a hospital bed that was nearly four hours across the state.

"Where do you want us to look? You need to rest."

"Didn't your mother need you?" Archer frowned at me, and I remembered why we'd come back in the first place.

"Does she?" Jude looked surprised.

"Simon– ah, said so. He found me after my—"

"Hissy fit." Archer supplied, the corners of his lips twitching. I shot him an evil look.

"Yes. That."

"Doubt it. Simon's been with me the whole time, except for fifteen minutes he went for a walk- oh." The pieces fell into place, and he looked between Archer and me with bright eyes. "Shit. Did he walk in—"

"Don't worry about it. Mom doesn't need me at all. Clearly. Where, Jude?"

He tossed me my brother's keys. "Top end. We got the fence fixed where Pierce was building sandcastles on the Black Hill side, but we only got as far as the river. From there to the other corner, well. We just haven't got the people to cover it."

"We got it."

Archer slipped the keys out of my fingers before I could protest, striding towards the battered pickup.

I thanked Jude, making him promise me he would rest, though I knew he wouldn't, and chased after Archer. Sliding in the passenger side, I barely got my seatbelt done up before he put the contraption in gear, bunny-hopping us down the road. Jude's laughter was audible from the house. He waved to us from the railing, then disappeared inside.

"Maybe he'll sleep," Archer muttered, crunching second gear.

"He won't. Sure you're qualified to drive this thing?"

"It should be in a museum."

"Damned right," I laughed.

He grinned back, squeezing my hand briefly, and at that moment, the tension between us dissipated. I settled back in my seat, closing my eyes.

When I opened them, we were at the river. I yawned, covering my mouth as I stared around. "The hell?"

"You snore." Archer never took his eyes off the track as he waddled the old vehicle over the stones and stopped on the other side of the river. "Actually, it's almost a purr. Sorta cute. This is as far as I go. You right to drive, kitten?"

"I am not a freaking kitten." I tapped his arm as he passed me the keys with a raised eyebrow.

"Is that right?" Archer took a step, leaning over with his arms on either side of my shoulders against the truck.

"Maybe." My voice dropped to a husky timbre. I bit my lip, heat flooding my cheeks as his eyes sparkled at me. He dipped his head, his lips a breath from mine.

Bark showered us from overhead. We both ducked, cowering behind the truck as the gunshot found us a second later.

"Jesus," Archer swore, reaching behind him. I frowned, but his hands came back empty. "Stay here." He pressed a firm hand to my shoulder, holding my gaze for a moment, then he slunk around the front of the truck.

160

Another shot ricocheted somewhere nearby, pinging off a rock, by the sound of it. I yelped, chasing after Archer, who collided with me at the front of the vehicle.

"I told you to stay where you were!" he growled, his momentum carrying both of us to the ground in the shadow.

"I thought you'd been shot!" I snapped, my hands checking over his chest and shoulders before I could process the fact that he wasn't acting like he was hurt.

"I'm fine, honey, but if you want to keep exploring..." His hands squeezed my waist, and my world narrowed for half a second. Then my brain returned.

"You're the one who stopped it all in the first place," I said tartly, sitting up.

"Did you really want Haldon watching us?" Archer asked, crouching next to me. He picked something out of my hair, a rueful smile on his face.

"What? Are you— Oh, my god. Wait. Is that who's shooting at us?"

"You fit a lot of questions in one sentence." Archer grinned, studying me. I glared at him.

"Are you kidding me?" I recalled the last time I'd said that to him, in his cabin, the impression of his lips still on mine as he hauled me upward. It seemed an age already. "Who's shooting at us?"

I picked the most important question first.

"Not us. I *think* they were trying to flush out the deer, herding them along the bottom of the cliff face, but it might not have been the most sensible approach. Nor the safest."

I peeked over Archer's shoulder, where one of our older farm trucks disappeared into the treeline, two shooters standing in the truck bed, their rifles aimed over the top of the cab.

"Oh, my god," I hissed. "I'll—" I was so furious at the lack of care factor that I couldn't get any further words out.

"I messaged Jude." Archer's fingers stroked along my back. "Let him deal with them. I know he's your friend, but that's his job, right?"

I clenched my teeth together so hard they ground against each other, breathing in through my nose, and finally conceded. "You're right."

"I know I'm right. God, you're beautiful when you're angry."

My eyes flashed to meet Archer's, my mouth hanging open. "You can't say something like that!" I squawked, "unless you want to start– start–" My mouth and brain jammed, nothing more coming out.

Archer's eyes darkened, their sparkle seeping into something different. "Don't tempt me," he said in a low voice, gripping my hand tight.

"What if I want to?" I asked, my voice so quiet I wasn't sure he would be able to hear me.

His hand gripped mine tighter, bordering on painful as he stilled. "Eve– God, girl, you have no idea how much—" His jaw snapped shut. "I'm not staying. And I don't want to break that heart of yours."

"You think highly of yourself," I snapped, not letting go of his hand. "What happened to a lonely woman and pent up energy?" I threw his words back at him, my heart aching already. His eyes hooded, staring deeper into me than I liked, and I knew he guessed too much.

"Oh, there's plenty of pent up energy," Archer grinned, though his eyes didn't lighten from their study of me, "but yours isn't the only heart, Eve."

He released my hand, turning his back to me, and pulled out his phone, his fingers moving fast over the screen.

I stared after him, my heart pounding.

The track to the back boundary bordered on the same cliff face we'd met Pierce on but in the other direction. I descended the eastern side of the foothills, then over the mountain itself.

"Are we going all the way over the mountain?"

I started humming *The Bears Go Over the Mountain.* Archer turned to me with an incredulous look. I giggled. "No. There's a gate, and the whole border is fenced off. Assuming it's held up," I frowned at the churned-up track in front of me. "Who the hell has been out here wrecking my tracks?"

"I'd say it's your young fellas yahooing their way across the property. Don't worry, Jude stopped them," he assured me.

"Thank god. I wonder if they're responsible for the barn door going too," I mused.

Archer shrugged, sending me a sideways glance, something dark in his expression that stopped me, but it flitted away within moments.

"Well, here's your gate. Closed and locked, by the look of it. The fence line looks good, too." Archer stopped the truck and jumped out, inspecting the wire. It twanged nicely.

The mountainside air stilled; warmth and cold swirled around my ankles in delicate eddies.

"We have to find those deer." I chose a flat rock sticking a few feet out of the pasture, looking out, but it wasn't high enough to see over the treetops. Not that it would matter if the deer were actually in the trees.

My toes tapped on the rock while I assessed my options. Looking for the deer inside the forest was a moot point — the chances of coming across them were less than nothing. But if I didn't get the little fellow inside the barn during the coming storm, I had no doubt in my mind we would lose him.

I shook my head, looking for something higher to stand on, but saw nothing — unless we went up the mountain. Then we'd be too far away to be useful to anyone. Okay, the deer were somewhere in the two bottom fields. But where?

Archer leaned against the truck, his arms folded.

"Well, you're useful," I grumped, then stared. I jumped off my rock, grabbing the truck bed, and swinging myself up. It gave me easy access to the roof from there, and soon I stood on top of the cab.

I stared out, missing my binoculars from my glove compartment. Trav hated the things, with little chance he'd have a pair.

"Where are we looking?" Archer clambered up beside me.

"There—" I pointed, highlighting the fences along the opposite ridge. "Where we drove the other day. It goes up to the top corner—"

"Where Black Hill Boy was destroying shit," Archer murmured, nodding. I snorted, tracing the outline of the ridge with my finger.

"—across the cliff, but I think there's little chance of seeing them there, what with the cowboys being idiots."

"They aren't usually like that?" Archer rubbed his chin, my eyes following his movement. He raised an eyebrow.

"No," I laughed at him, though my fingers clenched with a need to touch him. "Maybe they were drunk? They're definitely better behaved than that."

"Silly season."

I snorted. "Yeah, well, we don't usually get infected by that."

"Too far out of town?"

"Something like that." I bit my lip, searching the fields for the deer. A small cluster grazed in the yard behind the barn — Jude must have brought those in earlier. But the thick forest was impossible to see through.

"Eve, this is the river, right?"

Archer's arm pointed over my shoulder, the hairs on my neck rising at the near contact. I squeezed my toes in my boots to encourage blood flow to my brain.

"Yes," I said slowly, guiding his hand to the riverbed where we're crossed to where it disappeared into the cliff face. I'd always assumed it delved underground and had never been to see where it popped out on the other side. "Our land continues over the mountain and about a third of the way along the ridgeline. Pretty much the border to Canada."

I turned to show Archer and came up flush against his chest. His hands circled my waist briefly. With an unfathomable look in his eyes, he stepped back and jumped off the roof into the bed. The whole cab rocked precariously. I swayed with it.

"Whoa. Not a smart idea." I slipped down onto my backside and into the truck bed. "Why did you ask about the river?"

"Do they have a place they drink? Apart from their usual troughs, you put out?" Archer asked, rubbing the back of his neck. "Nah, that's a shitty idea. Forget I said it."

I stared. "Are you kidding me? That's a great idea! There's a little pool, sort of where the ground flattens out and the river slows. They've often been there. The water is still fresh, and it's close to where the river flows beneath the mountain."

Archer gave me a crooked grin. "Sounds like a goblin movie."

"Something like that. Let's give it a shot."

We trudged back along the track, and I took a path that led deeper into the forest. The canopy closed in, casting shadows over everything. I stopped the truck, sliding down from the driver's seat.

"It's a little walk in, but I didn't want to scare them in case you're right."

"I don't think I *am* right."

"Well, I've got nothing else, and I need to try so, be hopeful. Fake it 'til you make it, right?"

"Might have to be my new motto," Archer grumbled.

I paused. "Why's that?" I asked cautiously. He stopped just behind me.

"Because I keep doing weird-ass things on this damned property. Move, Eve." He poked me in the ribs.

I bit back a squeal, sending a quick elbow backward, which earned me a satisfying *oof*.

"Shh," I cautioned. "You don't want to scare anything."

I cast a cheeky grin over my shoulder. Archer rolled his eyes, clutching his ribs theatrically.

We heard the river early on, tinkling merrily in the stillness of the forest. Neither of us spoke as we approached the pool, crouching carefully behind a holly bush covered with berries and prickles.

I peered through the sparse foliage, only thick enough to create a small hide while still affording us a good view of the area. Nothing moved around the pool, its waters flowing smoothly from the mountain. Tomorrow, this area would likely be covered in snow; the river would be mostly frozen.

Shaking my head, I pressed my hands to my knees, preparing to rise. My knees ached, and I wanted to get home, though the fate of the fawn bothered me more than I wanted to show.

Archer's hand on my shoulder stilled me.

I turned my head the smallest amount, following the line of his nod. A dark coat spotted with white obscured our vision for a moment, then the small creature moved on. I let out a breath, watching the porcupine make its way across the undergrowth, pausing for a drink before it disappeared, wandering deeper into the mountain.

"Pretty, but not what we were here for. It was a good idea." I shrugged, suddenly exhausted, despite my nap earlier. "I really wanted—" Pressing my lips together, I turned back the way we'd come. Archer crashed through the holly bush, swearing prolifically. I grinned as I walked around it.

"Vicious damned thing," he growled, giving the shrub a death stare.

"Don't have those where you come from?" I asked with a grin. The death stare turned on me, but I didn't back down.

"Don't push it, Eve." Plucking leaves from his jacket, Archer walked to the edge of the pool, sliding his hands into the pebbles there.

"I wouldn't drink that. It might look pure, but you'll end up in a bed next to Trav's," I warned.

"I'm not drinking it." He sifted through handfuls of rocks. I shook my head, walking back up the path.

"Eve."

With a sigh, I turned back.

Archer swiveled on his heel from where he squatted on the riverbank, one boot in the water for balance where he'd been digging around in the rocks. It must have been icy, but he never said a word.

The man is hard as granite.

I wondered if I'd ever get beneath the surface of him. He gestured to me wordlessly, holding his fist out. I felt the weight of his gaze, assessing as he opened his hand, dropping a few small pebbles into my hand. Cold water trickled along my arm, inside the edge of my sleeve, and I bit back a yelp.

"Are you kidding? Would you stop—" I opened my hand. My mouth dried, and I couldn't say another word.

"Is this why Pierce is such a problem for Red Hart?" Archer said softly, pushing aside a few brown stones. He picked up a darker one, with a glossy finish, like glass. Holding it up, he let the dappled light of the forest highlight one of Red Hart's oldest secrets.

"How did you know?" I swallowed, unsure of how to approach this.

"Your mother's ring. She talked about it a few nights ago, after a little of the wine." Archer grinned, placing the luminous sapphire back in my hand. "Let's go find your deer."

He set off back down the track, and after a few moments of convincing my feet to follow him, I managed to get myself moving.

I caught up with him just before we reached the truck, turning over what to say in my head. When I reached Archer, he said nothing, just kept walking with a long stride. I kept up with him, half for pride, half from nerves.

"Keys," he murmured when the truck came into sight.

I passed them to him wordlessly, still clutching the few pebbles that were worth a month's income.

CHAPTER 9

I sat in the passenger seat, promising myself I'd stay silent. My determination lasted all of three minutes.

"We don't usually talk about it with—" I caught myself before I could insult him. "But we don't sell them very often, either. More of a back-up plan in case the ranch fails."

I flapped my hands uselessly.

"I've got no one to tell." Archer patted my fist; I looked down at those worn hands.

"You could have sold those and made half a year's pay. More…" My head tilted to the side, I watched him. His hands were easy on the steering wheel.

"Not mine to take."

"Because you don't need the money."

Archer's knuckles turned white. I knew that if I hadn't been watching for it, I would have missed it.

"Maybe I'm a secret millionaire. Wait—billionaire. That's the thing to be these days, right? I'm a sheik, traveling my way incognito around the US."

"Are you?" I sent him a grin, but it held no humor. "Maybe you could show me where you grew up? I'm running out of reasons to trust you, Archer."

"It's not me you should be worried about." His mouth clamped shut with an audible snap.

"Isn't it?" My question fell flat. I slid the uncut gems into my pocket. "Who am I supposed to worry about?"

The steering wheel creaked beneath Archer's hands. "Just look out for yourself, Eve." He pulled the truck up, his hand on the door to jump out and open the farm gate, but I beat him to it.

The air in the cab seemed constricted, and fresh air would be a nice change. At least I could trust it. Archer saw too much and said too little about himself.

Probably no more or less than any other drifter that passes through Red Hart.

I considered the thought, waving him through the gate, securing it with a padlock we didn't always use, but my faith in anyone right now had hit a pretty low point. Turning back to the truck, I was surprised to see a figure jogging toward us.

"Jude. What are you doing out here?" I asked in surprise.

"I've been trying to reach you. Or Archer. I found the fawn. And the mother. They're both safe in the barn. Little thing started exploring, and the mother seems to have settled. They're

179

good. The boys herded the bison back, too. Lucky, but all heads accounted for."

I grinned ear to ear. "You're worth every steak I've ever cooked for you. Don't you dare leave this place. Ever."

"Got no plan to." Jude scuffed his feet, his cheeks pink, not all of it from the cold or exertion. "So, you cooking tonight?"

"Always," I grinned back. Archer got out of the truck, turning to face us slowly. Jude paused, looking between us.

"Lover's tiff already?"

"You have no idea." I shook my head, digging the sapphires from my pocket and depositing them into Jude's palm. "Archer dug about for these in the creek bed. Suggested we go up to the pool and knew just where to look," I said lightly, letting the words hang with their own weight between the three of us.

Jude looked up, confusion and shock written on his face. "Shit. You don't happen to be a geologist in your other life, yeah?"

Archer laughed, but it sounded as strained as Simon's had been earlier in the day.

That was only this morning?

"What other life?" He joked, but it died away when neither Jude nor I laughed with him.

"You wanna walk back, or should I?" Jude muttered under his breath to me.

"Be my guest." I strode past Archer, glad to have some time to myself. "Good luck. And you need to talk to the young hands staying on about appropriate behavior. They almost shot us." I winked, and some perverse part of me enjoyed the shock value on his face as I passed him.

The sun dipped behind the mountain by the time I reached the big house. Or the clouds. In the last half hour, it had become difficult to tell. My legs ached. I cursed myself for being so full of pride — Jude would have ridden in the truck bed if I'd asked. My sore feet didn't really bother me. But I hadn't prepped anything for dinner for the hands, and some small part of me cringed as I realized it was Christmas Eve.

While our traditions ran to nothing more than an evening of tall stories and filled glasses paired with good, homemade food, I enjoyed the lead-up, usually.

Everything seemed different this year.

I stamped up the steps to the verandah, kicking mud from my boots and placing them in the box by the door. I prayed I'd remember to bring it in once everyone had left for the night, else we could all wake up to damp shoes come Christmas morning.

A voice around the side of the house stopped me as my hand hit the door handle. Inside looked so warm, and now that I'd stopped walking, the cold air took an icy turn down my collar. Huddling into my jacket, I walked quietly across the wooden boards, listening as I went.

"No, she's got no idea. I don't think any of them do." I recognized Archer's voice, clearly a private conversation on his phone. I turned to go back inside, but his next words froze me. "I'll take care of it, Ethan. Don't raise hell. This is my battle. Yeah, I shouldn't have left. Fuck off." The anger — *the rage* — in his voice was undeniable. Cold and clear, I witnessed a side of the man I'd been so close to for the last few days that he'd never shown here.

Until now.

I crept softly away from the corner of the house, hoping no one spotted me, and slipped inside the house, repeating Archer's words over and over.

I shouldn't have left.

This is my battle.

She's got no idea.

What the hell sort of man had I involved myself with?

This is why you don't sleep with the staff, Eve.

Maybe I should take a leaf out of Archer's book and tell that little voice to fuck right off.

Or maybe it was telling me all the truths I'd ever need to know.

A glass of red wine appeared in front of me. I took it, looking up into Simon's clear, grey eyes.

"I'm sorry about this morning. I shouldn't have followed you." He sent me a half-grin, shrugging. "I want to say that I was looking after your welfare when really I was hoping I hadn't lost you to another man."

His eyebrows wiggled, and despite myself, a small laugh burst out of my mouth.

"Oh, my god. Simon, you never had me. But thank you. I really did need that laugh today." I raised the glass to him, clinking it gently against his with a grin, and headed into the kitchen.

"I always aim to please," he called over the hubbub. I laughed again, shaking my head at his theatrics.

"He's a charmer." Mom cleaned a large kitchen knife, sliding it home into the block. "Now, Eve—"

"I did have a ham for tonight. But it might be a little late to put it on..." I hunted in the fridge but couldn't spot it. How does one hide a fifteen-pound ham shoulder from one's self? I shifted things, but the fridge simply didn't have enough shelf space to hide it.

A discrete cough at my shoulder interrupted my search.

"I put it on. Your mom gave me a little guidance. Hope I did it right?" Simon pushed a bowl of marinade in my direction. Next to me, a chopping board held a batch of glazed cherries in lines, all skewered on toothpicks.

"Wow, you're organized," I observed, dipping my nose towards the bowl. "And this smells amazing! What did you use?" I opened the oven, the ham sitting in the center, a diamond pattern cut precisely across it.

"Oranges, treacle, cardamon..." Simon listed a few herbs and something that ended suspiciously like *rum*.

Glaze shone lightly, and though it probably had another hour to go, it looked incredible. I shut the oven.

"I couldn't have done that well myself. Thank you." I smiled at the tall man, hoping he wouldn't read too much into it.

"Always a pleasure." He nodded to me, returning to the table where Jude was firmly ensconced next to Dad.

"Sit down," I motioned to Mom, "enjoy a rest."

"I rested all this week, Eve. I think the one who needs it most is *you*."

"It's Christmas Eve, and you expect me to stop? Are you sure you're part of this family?" I laughed at her.

She wound an arm around my waist. I blinked, sliding my arm around her shoulders. She was thinner than I remembered. When had I gotten too busy to notice that my mother wasn't holding up so well?

"Are you okay, Mom?" I asked softly, sliding the cutting board from beneath her hands.

"I'm fine, Eve. Now, we need candied oranges for the top of the brownies. If that nice young man didn't use them all up."

I rolled my eyes. "I'm sure we have bags of oranges. Which tray do you want?"

"The deep white Corningware one, please."

I dug around in the pantry, finally coming up with the tray she wanted. Mom's brownies were famous across our small area. And once you had one, you never felt the same about a brownie ever again.

Straightening, I wiggled still-sore-from-walking feet in my socks. I'd enjoyed it — I just wished it had been any other day of the year. I reminded myself to check on the fawn before I fell asleep tonight.

A shadow fell across the entrance to the pantry. I shook my head, filling the dish with oranges.

"Simon, this is becoming a bad habit. I told you—" I broke off as I looked at the man between me and my kitchen.

Archer stood in the space, making it look small with his broad shoulders, his feet set slightly apart.

"Eve, I wanted to say—"

"You're in my way." I walked right up to him, but he didn't move. "Please?"

"I want to know if we're good." His mouth opened, but nothing else came out.

"And?" I prodded, feeling rude at not at least hearing him out but unable to push the words of his phone call away.

"Jude slapped me on the wrist a few times."

"Is that all? He's not doing his job, then."

"His job is looking after you. I got death threats on that side of it."

"Did you?" I was surprised but pleased. Jude really was the extra brother Travis and I never had. "He's got his heart in the right place."

"So do you. You're not greedy. You try not to pry, and you spent all damned day looking for a baby and her mother when you obviously had things you would have preferred to be doing."

"That's a pretty long speech." I bit my lip, thinking back on my eavesdropping earlier. "I really do need to check on the deer after dinner."

"Can I come with you? I wouldn't mind checking that door, make sure everything's okay for the night."

"Archer, it'll be snowing by the time I go out there."

"I'm used to it."

"Yes, I'm sure you are. Arctic man, or wherever you're from."

"You got me there. Sheik of the Penguins."

I snuffed a laugh. "Here, give this to Mom. And be useful; pour yourself and Dad a drink. Please."

"Will do." He took the tray, leaving me empty-handed and completely bemused. Following him out of the pantry, I watched him laugh and dance with Mom, check with Jude which bottle of whiskey to pour, and take four glasses down to the table, sliding one across to Simon, though a moment of hesitation jarred his movement. Simon saw it, his eyes narrowing. Something darkened in them, and I was glad they were aimed at Archer and not at me.

His words rattled around in my head, then came the guilt over prying when Archer had made a thing out of my apparent lack of discretion abilities. Plus, I'd heard his words out of context, and I might not be the *she* he'd spoken about.

Having rationalized it to myself, I glazed the ham, waving Simon away the first few times I rotated it, brushing his masterpiece carefully while Mom worked on the brownie mixture.

"I'll get more eggs in the morning," I called over my shoulder to her.

"If they lay tonight. It's going to be frigid. I topped up the firewood in all the cabins today."

"I'm glad you got a walk-in." I swapped her spatula for a tea towel, lifting out trays from the top over we used more for desserts than anything else. "But I could have done that."

"While you were out chasing deer with your young man? Priorities, Eve." She smiled gently as she passed me the brownie tray, and I knew she meant no harm in it. I inhaled the chocolatey goodness on the way through, sliding it onto the second to bottom rack and set the timer.

"I think your ham is ready," I said to Simon, unsurprised when I turned around to find him standing inside the kitchen.

A small part of me rebelled; this was *my* space, and no one, apart from Mom, really came into it. That sounded childish, even in my own head, and I cast the thought away, though the irritation of having him in my space remained.

He held out his hand for the towel, and I shook my head. "Nope. You cowboys gotta be tough and do it barehanded."

"Right-o." Simon bent at the knees, making a show of rubbing his hands together and going through a small warm-up routine. Some of the hands gathered at the other side of the bench, laughing at his antics.

"Hurry up, or it'll burn," I hissed from the side of my mouth.

"Ahhh, there is only one thing to bolster my courage. A kiss from a fair maiden!" He swooped on me. I squealed amidst gales of laughter, slipping out from his hands. Simon put on a show of pouting, then made a beeline for Mom, kissing her cheek and waltzing her across the kitchen. I shook my head and waved a pair of oven mitts over my head.

"Has he earned them?" I yelled.

"YES!" The hands raised the roof, even Dad calling out. I presented the oven mitts to Simon, who bowed gratefully and presented the room with his roast.

The ham looked spectacular, filling the room with a mixed scent of citrus and salt.

"You've done yourself proud."

"Have to, in a place like this." Simon smiled, handing me a few cherries. Together, we decorated his masterpiece.

"A place like what?" I asked in surprise, my hand poised over the last cherry.

"Here." He turned to face me, his straight brow furrowed. "You really don't know, do you?"

"Know what?" I shifted under his assessing stare, his probing sinking too deep beneath my skin.

Simon turned back to the ham, fussing to put it on display in the dish. "All of you work so hard on the camaraderie, but this place, to them — you're their family. And the house, the mountain," he grinned, "you've gotta know it's spectacular."

"I do know," I said absently, watching the conversation at the table as everyone settled in with their drinks. Mom passed out baskets of bread rolls she'd headed, fresh butter on tiny plates placed between the men. "We need more women here. Just– the guys might like a bit of company. Wait that sounds really stupid."

"It's a community, Eve. You're up here on the borderlands. There's really no other place to be but right here. As for women, I'm sure they'd love some around." Simon's voice held a honeyed edge, while I held in a snort. If I brought women to work on the ranch, the place would be filled with new dramas. Well, more than we currently had. He pressed his hand over mine, stabbing the last cherry into the ham over the glaze. The aroma drew rumbles from my stomach. "Let's put this out."

"It's all yours."

Simon presented his Christmas Eve offering, carving, and plating it, carrying on several conversations at once. I nursed my wine, watching everyone as they cut into their food, glad to be away from everyone for just a moment.

He was right, though, I realized as I
watched the table. They were a family. My
family. Of Red Hart Ranch.

CHAPTER 10

I sent a message to Trav, a picture of the table and everyone at it, then deleted the thing before it could send properly. It felt mean, showing us around the table, enjoying each other's company when what I wanted was for my brother to be home with us for a full Christmas.

"Eve." Archer appeared before me as I scrolled through pictures of Trav as a child I'd scanned onto my computer when I'd made Dad's Christmas present. The antics of him on his first baby bronco being tossed high in the air bubbling laughter from me. Not a bone had been broken then.

"I miss my brother." I gave him a watery grin, ducking my head. His fingers curled beneath my chin, lifting my eyes back to his.

"He's your twin, honey. You're never going to be closer to him than anyone else."

"I'm not." Tears sprang to the surface. Where the hell had they come from? I peered over my phone at Archer. "It sounds like you know."

Something shuttered in him. "I've known a few twins. All peas in a pod. Not quite the same without the other." His gaze darkened. I looked back at my phone as he tugged my arm. "Sit down, Eve. You've been on your feet for hours."

I snorted. "Or my back."

Heat traveled up my cheeks as Archer laughed outright. "God, I'd forgotten that."

"What, me being on my back beneath you, or the comments Simon made afterward?"

I realized with a start, I hadn't forgiven the other cowboy for this morning. Archer's lips twitched.

"Which one doesn't earn me a slap?"

"Pick one." I sent him a grin, taking Mom's first tray of brownies out of the oven as the timer dinged behind me. Archer's eyes tracked the tray across the kitchen.

"Make sure you leave some room for that." I grinned at him and left the tray nestled in a bundle of towels to cool. Simon withdrew a pumpkin cheesecake from the fridge, and my mouth watered.

Archer dragged me over to the table. I sent a quick message to Travis with a promise to call him in the morning, guilt ribbing me as I enjoyed the company in the house without him. My time at the table didn't last long. The oven dinged again, Jude craning over my shoulder. I jabbed him lightly as I got up.

Mom's brownie was a hit. A treat that never failed, its chocolatey goodness towered a fluffy three inches high, stuffed with chunks of

white and dark chocolate. I served it into bowls
that disappeared quickly from the benchtop.

Silence fell over the house, the only sound
the clinking of spoons on plates as they
emptied. Mom winked at me. I toyed with my
own cube, the misshapen first piece I'd
extracted in a bid to cut the rest well.

Not that anyone would have cared, I
admitted to myself ruefully as plates made their
way back to the kitchen. Jude and Archer
bustled into my space. I stared at Jude in shock.

"You know not to come in here," I rebuked
him gently, spooning the brownie into my
mouth before either of them stole it. Unlikely,
but still... it *was* the last piece in the house.

"We're cleaning up," Jude announced,
turning me around and shooing me out of the
kitchen. *My* kitchen.

I spun in a circle and stomped back to
where I'd come from.

"Nu-uh. Staying. Out. Both of you." I fixed
the first one with a hard glare, then the other.

The other being Archer, who didn't look like anyone's glare would bother him. "Now, boys."

Jude shrugged, filling the sink with water. He jerked his head, and Archer stepped up.

"Come on, Eve. You've fed everyone. Now it's time for you to sit down and let us clean up for you."

I opened my mouth to object, and he grabbed the last bite of brownie from my bowl and stuffed it between my lips. I stared at him in surprise, the chocolate propping my mouth open, and made a muffled protest.

"Sit. Please?" Archer's hands found my hips. He turned me gently, pushing me out of the kitchen.

In something of a stupor, I swallowed my brownie, grabbed a bottle of water, and sat in Jude's empty chair next to Dad. He mumbled at me. I watched his lips, then his eyes jerking between the boys and me. I smiled, wrapping my smaller hand around his large one covered with age spots.

"They are good boys, Dad. We're lucky to have them."

Mom coughed and left us to it. Dad shuffled a bit more, adding his eyebrows to the mix.

"Mmm. I'm sure Jude will stay forever," I said with a smile, deliberately misunderstanding him. His eyes lit on me, and he hacked his coughing laugh. I shook my head, my cheeks reddening as he caught on. There were plenty of cylinders still firing up there, after all. His hand tightened around mine, and for all the joy in his tired eyes, I couldn't help letting the little whisper that rolled around my heart run free.

He won't stay here.

Predictably, we all drank too much. And after a few rounds of drunken carols, the hands flitted away to their beds, pressing kisses to Mom's cheeks, and helping Dad up to bed. Several drunken messages left my phone, and I hoped I'd sent the right ones to Trav and Rachel. Else Suzy might wake up to something a little odd in the morning.

Mom followed Dad up shortly after, and the ground floor emptied. Simon made up a batch of his mulled wine. I sipped my glass, my eyelids drooping.

Jude nudged me.

"Go to bed, Eve. I've got the livestock tonight."

"Are you sure? That would be a-ma-zing." I yawned behind my hand, my eyes watering. "Seriously, thank you. I'm spent."

"All good, babe. I'll check them now and come back to lock up after these two."

He nodded to Simon and Archer; the only ones left in the house. I nodded, exhaustion of the week hitting me like a sledgehammer, and followed him to the door, flicking lights off as I went.

The Christmas tree left a soft glow, covered in its fairy lights, and the ones Archer had decorated my garlands with did too, so for one night, I figured we could leave them on.

Archer followed Jude out the door, casting a look over his shoulder at me. His face was obscured by the dancing shadows, and I couldn't read his expression properly. I turned my glass in my hands, standing in the half-dark, and watched the boys walk across the yard to the barn.

"I thought it would be snowing by now," Simon spoke from so close behind me, I nearly lost my wine.

"My God, you scared me!" I hissed at him, stamping my socked foot on the floor, so I didn't kick him. My wine sloshed in its glass. I steadied my hand and took a hasty sip.

"That would have been a waste," he said, taking a step toward me.

"Um, yes." I went to sidestep him, but his hand shot out, catching my waist. "Simon—" I protested, batting at his hand.

"You did a great job tonight." He ignored me completely. "Amazing, the way you look after so many people but never yourself."

"Well, they did get me to sit down tonight. Albeit under duress." I grinned at the memory of Archer stuffing my face with brownie. "But I've been doing this all my life. I'm sure it's easier than it looks."

"It's not." Simon pulled me into him, bending into my space. I pressed my hands to his chest, a need to be clear about what I did — and didn't — want bubbling in my chest.

"How do you know?" I plucked his hand from my side, tapping his chest, and stepped back. The space gave me room to breathe. "Where are you from, Simon Haldon?"

"Your man isn't who he says he is." Simon took a step into my space again. I shook my head, adamant. "Maybe you should be asking him questions, more than me."

I do, but he doesn't answer them any more than you do.

The constant deflecting added to my exhaustion. Tired of wondering if I could have a love or sex life and not upset the entire ranch. At the risk of sounding like a petulant child, I refocused on the cowboy in front of me.

"He's not my man. I'm going to bed. On my own," I added.

Simon stood in the semi-darkness of the living room as I backed toward the stairs, not daring to take my eyes off him. With a short nod, he collected his hat and jacket and slipped out the door. Even with his boots on, he made little sound. I shivered, watching until I saw his shadow reach halfway down the path and sculled the rest of my wine.

I left the glass on the sideboard and ran quietly up the stairs, heading to my bedroom, but someone had beat me there.

Archer leaned against the doorway of my room.

I raised an eyebrow, halfway between pissed and amused. "I'm going to bed. On my own," I said, repeating the words I'd used with Simon only moments ago.

Archer unfolded his arms, grinning.

"I'm not here to proposition you, Eve."

"That's... sweet?" I asked. "Why are you here?" I said the words softly, not wanting to wake my parents. Archer nodded at their door.

"I checked on your Dad. I hope you don't mind. The younger men moved him and after their behavior today—"

"You were worried," I finished for him softly. He nodded. "Thank you, Archer."

Tears pricked the corners of my eyes at his kindness. I lifted tired arms, wrapping them around his shoulders in a huge hug.

"You're welcome," he murmured into my hair. "What did Haldon want?" He asked, drawing back.

I shrugged, turning to my door. "I don't know," I mumbled, the wine and exhaustion combining in an effort to knock me off my feet. "I don't care about him."

Archer was silent as I opened the door to my room, and for a moment, I badly wanted to ask him to stay with me for the night. Just to have someone to hold, to feel safe with. My isolation from my family, the distance of the ranch had never bothered me 'til this moment.

"Are you going to be okay?" he asked at my shoulder.

I nodded. "I need to go to sleep," I whispered, my neck beginning to ache.

Archer's hand covered mine on the doorframe, and he leaned into me. He reminded me of the forest paired with Dad's whiskey with undertones of cinnamon and spices. I remembered the moment on the outcrop when he'd done the fence run with me.

"Don't trust him, Eve." His rough voice grazed my senses, his deep timbre wrapping around me. "He's not what he seems."

That's what he just said about you.

I looked up over my shoulder at him. His gaze latched onto me, the single focus of his attention. It was both thrilling and overbearing at the same time. His words reminded me too much of my own.

"Neither are you," I snapped, uncomfortable with the feelings this drifter drew from me when I had no idea how to deal with them. "Don't think I didn't overhear your conversation. On the phone earlier."

His chin dipped, his dark eyes never leaving me. "Stay out of that, Eve. It'll lead to trouble."

"I'm not some southern belle who's going to do whatever you say." I yanked my hand from beneath his, turning to face him. My skin grew cold too fast. "This is my home. I'll look after it as I see fit."

A rueful grin spread across his face. I wanted to run my hands over his skin, to compare it against the rough quality of his voice. I shook my head; this drifter came from God knew where and this *couldn't* happen. Again.

"You're not southern," he murmured, catching a strand of my hair and curling it gently around his fingers, "but you sure as hell could be a belle anywhere." His breath brushed my lips, though I suspected I'd forgotten how to breathe. He was so close, my skin tingled with the need to touch him. I wanted his hands on me. He uncoiled my hair and dropped his hand. "Merry Christmas, Eve. I'll lock up for you."

He released my hand, dipped his chin once more to brush his lips over my cheek, and headed down the stairs with soft footsteps.

I waited until I heard the lock click at the door before I slipped into my own room, crossing straight to the window. Archer stood in the yard at the front of the house, his back to me. As though sensing me, he turned, looking straight up at me, pausing for a long moment. He placed his hat on his head and turned in the direction of his cabin, a clear invitation.

My heart beat loudly in my chest, blood rushing around my collar until I overheated. I watched until he disappeared between the trees leading to his cabin, desperately clinging to the desire to race down the stairs and into the yard.

But my traitorous feet refused to follow him.

CHAPTER

II

Ice crystals edged the window frame early on Christmas morning, creeping upward to meet the stalagmites dangling from the top. Round, smooth orbs sat at the base where condensation had dripped and refrozen, reflecting the yard outside upside down in a perfect inversion.

I awoke still half-dressed in my clothes from the night before. Maybe I'd been too tired, but I couldn't believe that I hadn't even bothered to get changed. Either way, my jeans dug into my hips, slightly swollen by too much wine and too much brownie the night before.

The sparkling ground outside reflected into my room despite the dark clouds still in the sky. Walking through virgin snow topped my seasonal list — even more so on a holiday morning. I knew I needed to check on the deer again and the new fawn. Having them freeze to death did not form part of my plan for a pleasant Christmas.

I wrapped myself in my blankets, making a giant meringue of myself, desperate to get up and start doing something for the day but not wanting to move from the warmth of my covers. My hands clenched them tightly. I wondered what would've happened had I followed Archer to his cabin last night.

A warmth that had nothing to do with my wrappings filled me from the center outward; Archer's touch on my skin burned into me. I closed my eyes, letting the feel of his mouth against mine close over me, a moment of selfish indulgence. But if he insisted on pushing me away, then I couldn't cling to his memory.

Launching myself out of my bed, I stripped off my clothes and headed straight into the shower Travis and I shared on the landing opposite Mom and Dad's bedroom. The steam cleared my head and allowed me to think things through before the ranch woke for the day.

Maybe Archer was right? Perhaps I *did* need to stay away from him. After Simon's reaction, I certainly didn't want any of the hands thinking that they could take advantage of the only young female left on the ranch. I missed Rachael's company dearly; Travis always had her around, and their flirting made me laugh.

Balls up, Trav, and ask her out already.

Although I didn't think that they'd slept together yet, I love my brother, and I would love Rachel as a sister-in-law too.

My head turned to the business side of things, running through with all the menu options for today. I had a lot of cooking to do. The older hands — like Jude — who had been around forever, often made up their own family favorites to remind them of the home that they either weren't welcome in or couldn't go back to.

Simon had got it right; Red Hart Ranch *was* a family home. And even if the family had no blood relations, we accumulated an amazing group of people on the edge of the borderlands. I slipped on my warmest pair of woolly bed socks, reasoning that today was a good sock day, padding slowly down the stairs.

The Christmas tree spread a benevolent glow over the entire downstairs area, lit from the night before. Beneath it lay an empty, red blanket. Even as adults, Travis and I had always run downstairs on Christmas morning, ready to unwrap the presents our parents had laid beneath the tree in the middle of the night. As we grew, that time got later and later. Probably more early morning, now.

We still loved the mystery and the enjoyment of Christmas morning. There was always something special about that first snow scattered across the ground. However, today it fell a lot heavier than it had in previous years.

A thick blanket of white lay over the yard and the fields behind it, pristine and unmarked with most of the herd locked away for the night. My breath smoked the window as I stared out, little rivulets of condensation tracing their own paths through it.

I shook my head; I was no more than a kid at this time of year, not a woman in her mid-twenties. My fingers brushed the needles of the spruce tree, studying faded handmade ornaments with bald patches where tinsel had worn away.

This year, the red cloth beneath the tree was empty. I clutched two small, wrapped presents for parents, others stuffed in my pockets for Jude, Archer, and Simon. I would cook for the boys this morning, so that would be their present from me.

It had been easy to buy for Jude as he needed a new belt buckle. Simon, I hadn't been sure of, but when I came across an unopened decorative tin of saffron and a tiny bag of Mountain Arnica seeds — Wolf's Bane — in the back of the pantry, I'd thought that the tall man might like it.

I felt bad that I haven't gotten him anything specific, but then I hadn't expected to have two drifters home for Christmas, either. Archer's present sat carefully in my pocket, and I tried to ignore the weight of it. I'd spoken to Dad about it, and he'd been happy in his way, croaking and nodding when I outlined my idea.

Pottering about in the kitchen, I flicked on the coffee machine, finding pastries Suzy had given me at the beginning of the week. Had Simon and Archer really only been with us for such a short period? I stared into my oversized coffee mug. It felt like they had both been with us for ages.

I unwrapped the flaky pastries with careful fingers. Suzy had done me proud, and though they were a few days old, they were still fresh-looking. And tasting. I licked the evidence from my lips as the first person entered the house for Christmas Day. Predictably, the other early riser was Jude.

"Merry Christmas," he called, his cheeks red, blonde peppering the dark stubble on his chin. Something sounded off in his tone, though I couldn't quite pick it.

"What's up?"

"Ah, nothing. Well, sort of. The barn door got left half ajar this morning, and the fawn must have slept too close..." Jude trailed off, unable to finish his sentence. I peered closer at him. Not only were his cheeks red, but his eyes were rimmed in red, too.

"Why was the fawn moved?" I asked. He spread his hands wordlessly. "Jude? Did we lose her?"

He nodded, opening his arms. I stumbled into them, clutching his jacket.

"You'd think after nearly two decades of this shit, it'd get easier."

"Not when it's something so young we have looked after since its birth. Stupid, out of season thing." I stubbed my toe on the floor and got Jude's shin by accident. "Oh. Sorry."

He grunted. "Thanks, Eve. Don't ever carry a grudge with me, okay?"

"Sorry." I backed away with my hands wide in surrender. The door creaked, and I wiped my eyes in a hurry. "I need to keep going with... this." I waved my hands at my excuse.

Jude blinked tiredly, then put on his best pretend face for the day. I sighed, wondering if I could be bothered to make an effort this year. Everything just seemed to be going wrong, and my energy would run dry if I had to continue with the *fake it 'til you make it* attitude.

The kitchen filled with warm buttery scents, and behind me, Jude's belly rumbled.

"That smells good. If I eat any more, I'll look like Santa. Coffee?" he asked with a hopeful face.

"All yours." I passed him a steaming mug as the door opened again. "Close that," I called, pretending to shiver.

"You're tougher than that." Archer appeared at the door too quickly.

"Don't you bring those boots in here!" I yelled across the room, flapping my hands. "I don't want the cold side of Christmas in here with us."

"Yeah, sorry." He kicked the offending objects off beside the door and trumped in on his socks. "Merry Christmas, Eve." He wrapped me in a bear hug, pressing a kiss into my hair. My cheeks flushed with heat until my face matched Jude's.

I leaned into him, hating that I craved his hands on me but curving to his touch despite my resolutions not to. Cold patches covered my back as he dropped his hands. I busied myself, making him a coffee, placing the cup into his hands.

"Merry Christmas to you, too."

He stood there for a moment, looking at me. I shook my head with a smile, waiting to see if he said something, but he just sipped his coffee. Jude coughed.

"Ah, shouldn't you check the oven, Eve?"

I sent the foreman a grateful smile, whirling to check my pastries. They glowed golden and crisp.

"Perfect," I murmured, my attention focused back on making food for everyone. The cowboys began to filter in as I laid platters on the table filled with chantilly cream, pastries, and jams. Another held bagels I'd been saving and covered bowls of eggs and bacon to keep them warm.

Holly completed the table, sprigs Jude went back into the cold to fetch for me sitting jauntily between the serving plates. Cinnamon quills and star anise lay scattered between them. The tiny pile of presents in the center grew, overflowing between the decorations.

I smiled as the chatter rose, filling the rooms as Mom made it downstairs. I made her favorite tea, a warm, spicy one of red berries and black leaves, and gave her a hug. She squeezed my shoulders, sliding a small gift into my hands. I hugged her again.

"Is Dad not coming down?" I flicked the coffee machine on again. It was getting a workout this morning.

Mom shook her head. "I think he'll sleep in a while longer."

I nodded, letting Jude pull her away, knowing he'd feed her, but sent him a long look, hoping he'd get the message and not mention the fawn to her. Biting my lip against the cramp in my chest, I looked down the long table and noted more than one seat empty. Aside from Dad and Travis' spots, Simon was also absent from the table.

I placed my presents in front of the boys and Mom and offered gingerbread coffees to the rest of the table. Counting the *yeses*, I whipped cream, putting out tall glass mugs and layering the coffees as best I could without the lot getting cold. The table got quiet again as everyone ate, and I smiled, finishing my own coffee though it had lost its heat long ago. I stoked the fire and then slipped in between Jude and Archer.

Jude gave me a one-armed hug, and though Archer didn't look at me or break his eating stride, the corner of his mouth turned up, just a little. I stared at the firelight reflecting from the deep reds in his hair.

"Do I have something in my beard, Eve?" he asked softly, still not looking at me. I flushed again.

"No." I turned to my own plate of food. "But I wouldn't go so far to call *that* a beard."

He laughed. Cold blasted my back. I shivered, turning my head, but I already knew who was missing from the table.

Simon stepped bootless into the house, putting his hat up on the rack. Snow dusted the floor beneath it, and I realized it had started snowing again.

"I should check the rest of the herd," I said quietly, tears lodging in my throat. I started to stand and found two hands on my back, pushing me down.

"Sit," Jude said firmly. "I've got this."

Archer rose as well, squeezing my shoulder. His fingers lingered on my back, and I heard him talk softly to someone behind me. The two men departed. I sat alone, chewing my pastry with empty space on either side of me. The bench shifted as a body filled the spot on my left.

"Merry Christmas, Eve." Simon kissed my cheek in a swift movement before I could react, placing a slim, wrapped present in front of me. I looked at him in surprise.

"You didn't have to do that." I extracted his present from the pile and placed it in front of him.

He raised an eyebrow. "Neither did you."

"True."

We unwrapped them together. A collection of turquoise beads strung on a thin leather throng formed a bracelet that tumbled into my hands. I blinked at Simon.

"Thank you. You really didn't have to—"

"It's a small thing. One of the boys traded with a traveler in town a few weeks ago, and I managed to convince him to part with it."

I grinned. "Do I want to know how?"

Simon shook his head with a small smile that hinted at a secret kept. "No." He took the bracelet from my fingers, sliding it over my wrist. He turned my hand, wrapping his much larger one around it, smooth and long-fingered. "It suits you."

I studied the turquoise beads, the black lines running through them reminding me of

Montana's incredible river system. "It's beautiful. Thank you."

"Like you. Thanks." He waved the little seed pouch before me when I protested. Shaking my head, I explained what they were used for.

"I have to get started for the day." I half rose when he stopped me with a hand on my wrist.

"Don't you ever take time off?" He sent me a small smile that I was sure would have heated panties halfway across the state.

Not mine.

I considered his question, frowning.

"To do what?"

His laughter followed me to the kitchen. I cleaned up, then remembered to call my brother, bouncing up the stairs on a caffeine-fueled high, searching for my phone, but it wasn't where I'd expected. Maybe I'd left it downstairs? I flopped on my bed for a second, movement catching my eye outside my door.

224

I frowned, my over-full belly preventing my first attempt to get off the bed. I groaned, considering loosening the button on my jeans, and had another go, this time, a successful one. Stretching, I stepped into the corridor. Nothing moved. I shrugged, hoping the ghost of Christmas past or future wasn't haunting us to add to the semi-controlled chaos of the ranch.

Warmth blasted me as I made it downstairs, the hands filtering back out the door. I raised an eyebrow at Simon, eating his way through the table alone.

"Poker tournament, I believe," he said around a mouthful of croissant.

"They know they can do that here. It's not a workday for them. Or you," I added, my thoughts turning to Jude and Archer. Jude didn't really take weekends much at all. He seemed to love working and keeping busy and had been that way for years.

A pang hit my chest as I hoped his wouldn't be the next empty seat at the table any time soon.

Archer appeared down the stairs, adjusting his belt. I left Simon to his food, frowning, remembering the shadow in my doorway. "I thought you were out in the yard with Jude?"

His dark gaze lit on me, his hand curling around my upper arm as he drew me around to the small sitting room behind the kitchen and pantry. This side looked up to the foothills of the mountain. Though pretty, it didn't have the same effect as the view from the verandah at the front of the house. The kitchen cut out the usually-noisy area of the house.

"I went to check on your Dad."

"Thanks?" I asked, with a small frown. "Is he okay? I thought I saw someone up there, but... the landing was empty." I let my words hang between us.

The corner of his mouth quirked. "It got busy. I thought he might want to come down, but he was pretty out of it."

"You really don't need to do that, you know."

Archer nodded. "I know. And... I wanted to give you this." He placed a small figure in my hand, wrapped in nothing, and closed my fingers around it.

His eyes traced the bracelet on my wrist, but I was grateful when he said nothing.

I opened my hand to reveal a tiny deer carved from what looked like a much larger piece of bone, or hirn. I ran my fingers over it. The smooth surface glided beneath my fingers, where he'd polished it. The antlers were perfect, and between them, he'd managed to carve Red Hart's logo. I blinked back tears that rose to the surface as I turned the tiny figure over.

"This must have taken you hours."

"Since I got here," he agreed. I raised my head.

"What?"

"As soon as I got here, I knew what I wanted to use that last section for, but when I started, I got the idea it wasn't something I'd keep. Something that was meant to be yours."

I stared at him, my mouth half-open. Archer stood still, watching me. A lesser man might have fidgeted, patted his head, or bounced from foot to foot with nerves. Instead, Archer's calm crossed the area between us. He watched me, unembarrassed from such a huge statement.

To me, at least.

"This is... amazing. I had no idea you were so good." I grinned. "I should commission you to do something for the living room. Something bigger."

"If I had the time." Archer's head shook, just a little. "I can't stay, Eve. You know that."

"I know," I whispered, swallowing past the lump in my throat.

You never get involved with any of them like this.

Archer stepped forward, raising his hand to slide beneath my hair. Every movement was perfectly controlled, slow, giving me time to back away.

I don't want to back away.

My heart pounding inside my chest, I stepped into him as his arms closed around me. The hand at my neck molded to the back of my head, tugging gently in my hair until I tilted my head back.

Then he kissed me.

Archer's mouth pressed gently against mine, his lips soft but firm, skillfully opening my mouth with his before he angled his mouth over mine, deepening the kiss. I moaned against him. His tongue stroked mine, sliding inside to taste me.

A flush of warmth pooled deep inside me. My hands slid along his arms, finding the curves of his shoulders until they were around his neck. He pulled me into him so close that if he hadn't been holding me up, I would have fallen.

But he wouldn't let me fall.

Every hair on my arms stood on end, a shiver wracking me as his arms tightened around me. A controlled urgency coiled tight within him, released an inch at a time.

I wondered what Archer would be like if he let that control go.

When he drew back just enough to break the kiss, my chest rose and fell with long, deep breaths, my eyelids heavy as I opened them to look at him.

"I can't stay," he repeated, his voice soft enough that only I would be able to hear him, "but I can make memories with you. If you'll let me."

He studied me, and deep inside those eyes, I could see the tiny seed of fear I knew no one else would ever notice, a part of himself I guessed he rarely shared with anyone, if at all.

"I'll let you," I whispered, reaching up on my toes to kiss him again. His hand tightened on my waist, and I wondered if we wouldn't end up sprawled on the floor in the house if I didn't step away. I took a deep breath. "Stay here?"

Archer's head inclined in a small nod. I shook my hair out, hiding a smile as I headed back to the living area. I collected his gift from the table — the only one left — and walked back to him, my cheeks warm. I turned the present over in my hands, suddenly unsure if I'd missed the mark with him.

His eyes tracked me as I entered the small room. He hadn't moved. I placed the wrappings in his hands and stuffed mine in my pockets so I wouldn't fidget. Archer looked from me to the present, his brow furrowing for a brief second before he shook it away with a smile.

"Thank you." He unwrapped the gift with sure movements, taking care with each fold while I tried not to jiggle my feet.

The wrapping fell away, and he stared into his hand. I swallowed, biting back the urge to break the moment with my chatter.

Archer wound the black leather strap around his fingers, running their rough pads over the well-worn silver that capped the old arrowhead. The leather was reasonably new; Dad had reworked it only a few years ago, but

it had barely been worn and sat in a box in his
room ever since.

Archer said nothing, tracing the edge of the
arrowhead with his thumb.

"Dad found it by the river. Years ago. We
had a drifter," his mouth curled up at the
words, "come through who worked silver, and
he made this up for us. Carted a lot of stuff
around behind him." I shook my head at the
memory.

My hair fell over my eyes. I pushed it back,
startled to find Archer right in front of me.

"You don't have to give this to me, Eve. I'm
no one."

"Well, that's bull—"

I never got to finish my curse before he
kissed me again, sending my head and every
sensibility swimming. I ran my fingers over his
cheeks, loving the sharp scrape of stubble
against my palms. His arms wound around my
waist, lifting me into the air as he kissed me.

232

Archer put me down gently. I took the lariat from him, slipping it over his head.

"I love your hair," I murmured, fixing his collar.

He slid the silver piece to a comfortable length at the front of his shirt, bending to brush his lips over my cheek. Shivers raced along my arms. "Have I said thank you properly yet?"

I shook my head, grinning. "Not yet."

"Minx."

He kissed me again. This time, I sank into him and entirely forgot how to breathe.

CHAPTER 12

I finally remembered to call Travis around midday. My head seemed both empty and full at the same time. Jude took pity on me, opening the barn doors to let the animals out into the small field near the house. If the weather closed in again, we could always get them back in and with a lot less work, this way.

My phone had resurfaced in the pantry. I had zero memory of putting it there, but honestly, my mind had been pretty frazzled the last few nights. I hadn't even checked the website shop where we sold our products and took inquiries or sent out a newsletter for Christmas from the ranch...

Tapping my forehead with my phone, I groaned, staring out the window. The snow sparkled on the bank behind the house. I desperately wanted to go for a walk through the forest before anyone else, only a stretch of untouched snow before me.

My indulgence. A moment of peace before work resumed.

It was one of those things of living off the land; actual months and dates — apart from bigger holidays like today — had little impact on us. Instead, we worked around the weather cycles, which shifted just a little, year by year.

Sighing, I hit call, and after a moment, Travis' face popped up on the screen.

"Evie!!" He yelled, struggling upwards. Rachel's face appeared beside his, grey bags under her eyes, her hair mussed around her face.

"Oh, my God, Rachel. Tell me they gave you a bed!" I half-yelled. "And Merry Christmas!"

"Merry Christmas!" They chorused back, both breaking into giggles. I didn't bother to hide my smile.

"How are you feeling? What do they say?" I broke over them. "Are they feeding you both? Do I need to come down there?"

"Hell no!" Travis yelled back. Rachel broke up into gales of laughter, disappearing from the screen though I could hear her snorting in the background.

"Alright then." I grinned at him. "Seriously, how are you? Miss you like hell."

"Miss you too, Evie." Trav gave the screen a sloppy kiss. I grimaced then paused as Rachel reappeared on the screen. I studied their faces; both bore red noses.

"Are you two drunk?" I asked incredulously.

"The nurse brought around Christmas wine." Trav rubbed his nose.

"And another brought champagne. So we sorta kept them both."

I raised my eyebrows. "What about your pain meds?" I asked Trav. He shrugged, ignoring me. Typical. "Are they working?"

My twin rolled his eyes. "Yes, Eve."

Rachel snorted quietly into her hand. My eyes narrowed. I opened my mouth, but Trav cut me off.

"How's Dad? And Mom?"

Guilt instantly assailed me. I should have invited them to the call. "I'll get them."

Trav shook his head. "I'll call you later. That's not what I meant."

"He's... okay? Honestly, he's pretty good. Sleeps a lot, but good." Even I was surprised by my positivity. "He's talking in grunts and coughs, but I can understand him. He laughs a lot, and... the mind is still there, Trav."

He stayed silent for a long moment, staring at something beneath the screen, and when he looked up, his eyes were glazed. "That's good," he managed to get out, and instinct — our twin instinct — told me he was holding back something fierce.

Rachel jumped in, her hand on his good leg, quite high up. "That's great!" she said, a little too brightly. The screen moved. She seemed to have taken the phone from Trav's hands. Snowy white filled the screen behind her.

"What the hell are you doing, babe?"

"Getting away from the nurses," she muttered, "hang on."

A lurid green filled the screen behind her.

"Where are you? Is that the hall?" I yelped.

"Shhh." She cautioned. "Your brother is at the mercy of a strict nurse and her assistant. The others are amazing," she rolled her eyes," I swear the skirts get rolled, and buttons pop when they walk into Trav's room."

"You need to claim the boy," I said firmly, wishing I'd made another coffee. My eyes closed as my head tilted back. "Or someone else will."

"I'm doing my damnedest, Eve. Honestly. I don't think his eyes wander, but..."

"How often does he come to you? He chose our Christmas tree from your property, the same as he does every year." I protested.

A glass of chilled champagne appeared in my hand. I tipped my head back. Simon stood behind me, his grey eyes hooded as he stared down at me. I smiled.

"Thank you." I raised my glass to Rachel on screen, and she giggled. "Oh, my god. You guys really are done, aren't you?"

"Just a bit," she snorted again. I laughed outright.

"Uh-huh." Bubbles fizzed on my tongue. Heaven. I wondered what Simon had opened.

"Who's he?" Rachel giggled again.

"Drifter. Ask Trav. He brought him home."
In my peripheral vision, Simon wiggled his ass.
I suppressed a giggle but felt bad; I sounded as
though my brother had brought home a stray
dog.

"Promise. Okay. I'll call you next time."
White walls washed past Rachel as she jogged
back to my brother. "They need me. I'll call
you. Merry Christmas!" she shouted into the
phone and hung up. I held the phone in my
hand, silent, and prayed my brother was alright.

I'd forgotten to tell him about the fawn.

By the time I'd prepped lunch and dinner
meats, the boys had started bringing their own
contributions for the table up to the big house.
One of our regular drifters, if there was such a
thing, brought his Mother's Gumbo. Cage put
it on the table. I wafted the steam towards me
appreciatively.

"I've missed that." I rose, hugging him. "And what's this?"

This was a new hand I'd seen briefly in the last few days, who presented me with a green bean casserole. He wouldn't look at me, preferring to study my boots. I thanked him as Cage slapped him on the back of the head, rolling his eyes as he towed the nervous boy down the table.

Predictably, Simon wanted to cook something of his own, and I gave him free run of the kitchen, albeit reluctantly after putting my own contribution — a chocolate meringue pie — into the fridge. There were a few pastries leftover from breakfast, and I took some up to Dad, glad to see him awake. I placed his present before him and kissed the top of his head. Mom had disappeared, and I hoped she managed to get some time to herself outside amidst the hubbub of the house.

His thick fingers struggled with the paper, tremors rippling through them. I gave the little tugs from the corners, and it came apart easily. Dad flicked through the short, fat pages of the photo book I'd printed off for him. I'd gone back as far as I could into his younger years, traveling through a lifetime of ranch life, watching as he grew it from a smaller building into a larger homestead. Mom arrived, and then Travis and I were crawling about the yard in onesies, posed on the backs of unimpressed deer.

Dad grunted, snorting at the pictures in his garbled speech. I nodded, giving him a running commentary as best I could of Red Hart's history through Dad's eyes.

He managed to finish his cup of tea. I poured him another, catching it when his eyelids began to droop. Slipping off the bed, I tucked him in. His hands clutched the book opened to a picture of Mom, heavily pregnant with us. Pain clenched my chest, and I left a little piece of my heart in the room with him. I made it outside the door before the tears started. Leaning against the wall, I gripped the teapot too tight, my eyes flooding with tears that cascaded over my cheeks.

Snuffling, the pot slipped in my hands. I caught it, but the tiny lid popped out of its place and landed with a clunk on the floor. Muttering curses softly to myself so I wouldn't wake Dad, I picked it up. Miraculously, only a small chip off the decorative knob at the top was the extent of the damage. I collected the broken china and went back downstairs for more coffee and some super glue.

I wiped my tears away before anyone could spot me, though I knew my face would be puffy from my ugly cry. The teapot went back together quite well. Impressed with my own handiwork, I studied the join, not being much of a craftsperson.

"What happened to it?" Mom asked, surprising me. She took the lid from my hands, inspecting it with a nod.

"I dropped it. But it's an okay fix."

"It's just fine. Why don't you go outside? The snow has stopped for now, and you should go out before it starts again."

"You think we'll get more?"

Mom made me a cup of coffee, and I took it gratefully.

"I do," she said, giving me a hug. "And your Dad and I will be just fine."

I nodded, my eyes filling with tears again. I rarely showed this much emotion; it didn't help the ranch run, and my head kept forming disjointed thoughts, the distractions too much for my short attention span. Maybe I did need that walk before the house filled with people again.

"Thanks." I hugged her again and took my coffee outside, stopping to get my coat and boots from their place near the door. I grabbed a beanie as well and stepped into the yard.

Mid-morning and I hadn't left the house until now. I shook my head; this year definitely didn't have the same feel as other years. White crystals reflected brightly beneath a white sky. The effect was blinding. I snuggled into my jacket, glad I had left my hair out, and perched the beanie on top.

The barn was empty of animals and people. I wandered around the top field but couldn't spot any of the herd. With the loss of the fawn sitting heavy on me, I needed to check the rest were okay. The paddock by the barn led into another, larger field, covered in trees at once corner.

I slipped through the gate, fresh snow sliding beneath my boots, not compacted enough yet to crunch. The grounds sparkled in the brisk air, pristine and silent. Perhaps the boys were all involved in that poker game Simon had mentioned.

Heading for the trees, I made my way across the field; the snow covered my boots to my ankles. It hadn't been the heavy snow we'd been warned about. Maybe it would turn up in a day or two. Or maybe the local doomsayers had been wrong, after all. Above me reflected a pale pink hue, touched with grey and lit from beneath; a rose quartz sky.

I sipped my coffee, the thermos retaining its warmth. The rush of hot liquid in my chest contrasted with my icy cheeks and fingers. Maybe I should have put on some gloves, too.

A sense of quiet hung over the ranch, and for just a few minutes as I crossed to the copse of evergreens, I was the only person on the grounds. For the first time in days, my chest opened, allowing in deep breaths of the fresh air.

Maybe I'd dealt with too many people? The ranch often got busier throughout the year, and it had never bothered me before.

I shrugged the thought away, not wanting anything to ruin my Christmas day.

The trees were covered with a good layer of snow. It dangled from the branches, clumps sat on top of the broad limbs, but at the tips, each needle was coated in a fine spray of snow, giving the entire copse a frosted green look.

I peered into the trees, but the snow-covered trees shrouded the copse in darkness. A flicker of movement deep within drew my gaze. A branch caught my shoulder, ice sliding down the inside of my shirt. I squeaked a little too loudly for the serenity of the crisp air, and deer erupted around me in a flurry, bursting out of their place nestled beneath the trees.

"Nice moves."

I swore, backing out. My thermos was taken from my hands. I nodded my thanks as my beanie tumbled into the snow. "Damn." I shook it out, the woolly material too damp to be of any use. Stuffing it inside my jacket pocket, I tried to straighten my hair but gave up after a moment of trying to straighten the wayward strands intent on doing their worst. "I'm a mess."

"A hot mess, though." Archer handed my coffee back, slipping his hands into his pockets.

"I'm not quite sure that's how that term is meant to be used."

"No? Well, I'm a bit out of it." He fell into step with me, walking around the trees and further into the forest. I wasn't quite ready to go back to the house yet.

"Not used where you're from?" I asked, staring straight ahead.

Archer sent me an amused look. "Will you give up?"

"Nope."

He laughed, the warmth of the sound filling me. I looked over my shoulder, counting the rusty colored heads against the silver-frosted ground. A few of the herd cuddled together, peaceful. I smiled.

"They've survived well," Archer commented, following my gaze. "Jude let them out this morning."

"These ones have." I bit my lips, glad the tears didn't make another appearance. "Sorry. It's just—"

"There's no reason to be sorry, Eve." Archer's gaze stayed steady on me.

"You've been a huge help, especially with Trav away. It's a relief," I confessed, the list of things I had left to do hitting me. "Oh, hell. I haven't done the newsletter or anything." Turning on my heel, I wheeled to face the house.

Archer caught my elbows, swiveling me back. "You need to stop. Enjoy it, Eve." He picked leaves out of my hair, attempting to straighten it, but gave up after a minute. I sent him a rueful smile.

"Okay. For half an hour. Or until I run out of coffee."

"That last caveat isn't fair," he argued, "You're like a camel with that stuff."

"What an attractive image."

He snorted. "Yeah. Maybe not the best one."

We wandered into the forest, the sky becoming green underleaves, though the snow had made it to the path beneath.

"It's so beautiful. I never get tired of seeing the ranch like this."

Archer's hand found mine, enclosing me in its warmth. He squeezed gently, pulling me closer to him as we walked. We reached a stream that had broken off from the main river, trickling down the hillside from the hills above. The edges had a matte sheen where the slower moving water at the sides had frozen, but the center still ran, tinkling merrily.

Archer pulled me into his arms when we stopped, propping his chin on my head. I finished my coffee, leaning back against his chest, reveling in the solid mass of muscle.

"I want to know who you are because otherwise, I won't know who to remember.' I said softly, turning my cheek to press against his shirt. He stroked my hair, tangling his fingers in it. "If you're trying to fix that, I'll tell you now, there's no hope."

"Nah, gave up on that ages ago. But I'm not giving up on you." He turned me to face him, wrapping his fist in my hair, tugging me closer. "I'm who you see now. Not anything from before or who I might be when I leave."

I stared at him, unsure of how to answer him. "How do you live like this?" I asked in a whisper, unable to fathom his life, his lack of stability. "What is it that means you can't stay?"

"I'm here now," was all he would say before he dipped his head, kissing me slowly until every thought left my head, except for one I'd been asking myself since the day he'd arrived at Red Hart.

Who are you, Rhys Archer?

CHAPTER 13

I finally pressed send on the newsletter that had been bothering me for the best part of three days. Sitting back, I rolled my shoulders. Tension popped in knots across my back. Collecting my phone, I powered down my computer.

My phone kept vibrating with pictures from my brother and Rachel in various poses. Both of them had a dry wit, Rachel easily the more outgoing of the two. I was glad Travis had her for company when he must be so down, away from the ranch.

Another photo came through of the two of them. Rachel had a candy cane between her teeth, draped across Travis' lap, battling with the enormous white fake beard hanging over her head attached to my brother's that looked like he might have stolen it from the ward Santa.

I collected my teacup from a few nights ago, and, finding it empty, I refilled it with fresh water from the bathroom, swirling the dregs in the bottom. Bitter leaves caught in my throat. I coughed, admitting it had been a bad judgment call, and headed for the stairs to refresh my cup.

I yawned, making my way downstairs one slow step at a time. I could do with another caffeine hit to tide me through the rest of the day. People bustled around the ground floor, rushing around me, but my energy appeared to have deserted me for the day already. My steps were stunted, moving me in slow motion.

The table had been cleared as I passed it in my daze, and when I finally looked up, the kitchen was full of people. I watched them from a bemused distance. A shadow stepped in front of me.

Archer took my cup and travel mug from me with a concerned look on his face. His hand wrapped around my arm, and he guided me back to the table.

"Sit down, Eve."

I sat, not thinking to argue with him. "There are people in my kitchen." It was lunchtime. The penny dropped. "I need to serve lunch."

"We've got it. How are you feeling? You weren't like this before."

He took the chair opposite me, leaning his elbows on his knees as he studied me. My teacup dangled from his large fingers.

"That looks ridiculous," I snorted, beginning to laugh.

Archer's arms slipped around me, pulling me against his shoulder as he shushed me. I leaned into him, my laughter ceasing abruptly. I frowned, trying to think it through but my eyes shuttered closed on their own. I fell asleep on Archer's shoulder, amusing myself with the lines on his checked shirt.

To find a different shirt and a very different smell under my nose.

"Eve. You're drooling on me."

I shifted, Jude's eyes coming into focus above mine. He patted my head, nudging me up. I rubbed my eyes. "Why am I sitting at the table?"

"You came in zoned out as hell. The boys made Christmas lunch. You've had rest, which you obviously needed."

"Oh." It was Christmas. "Oh, hell," I groaned, my head splitting. A glass of water floated before my eyes. I straightened, taking it from Archer's hand. He nodded over my head, and Jude vacated his seat. Archer slid into it.

"Are you okay? I worried about you for a bit."

"I'm fine. Honestly. It's just... it's been stressful. Everything must have caught up with me." Archer stared at me and said nothing. "What?"

He held my gaze for a moment longer, his lips pressed together. "I'm allowed to worry about you."

"For now," I countered. *Until you leave.* A plate of crisp, golden sweetness slid onto the table in front of me. I inhaled a mix of Christmas spice and honey. "Oh, my God." I looked up into the eyes of a young cowboy who had only been around for a few weeks. "Kyle, is it?"

He nodded, his cheeks reddening. "Yes, ma'am."

"Archer, move over," I said, not looking at him. "This young man has to tell me all about how he made this. And maybe write it down?" I asked hopefully, not trusting my sleep-addled brain to recall anything important at this point. I popped one of the crisp balls into my mouth and moaned.

"Steady on, there." Archer rose as I'd requested, squeezing my shoulder. He held on just a minute longer, and Kyle looked up, nothing short of terror on his face as he shuffled around to explain his creation to me.

Once I'd extracted the recipe from him and had his promise to dictate the recipe to me — the young man wasn't confident of his handwriting abilities — I tried the various dishes overpopulating the Red Hart Ranch table. The hands had done us proud, Jude even knocking out his own bean stew. A once-per-year occasion and well worth the wait.

Groaning, I rolled away from the table, making sure the boys knew I needed their recipes. In the back of my mind, I'd been adding to the recipes I'd collected over the years. I wanted to make an RHR cookbook, something similar to what I'd done for Dad, but for the ranch, all the hand's favorite home-cooked meals they'd been willing to part with as they passed through over the years. I added recipes to my book every Christmas; to me, food and family went together, even if you weren't related.

I caught sight of Archer's blue and white checked shirt as he leaned against the railing on the verandah outside, talking to Jude.

Or weren't around for very long.

I excused myself, letting everyone mill around the table. Lunch and dinner were an informal affair; usually, we just kept putting food on the table and rolled over from one giant meal into another.

Then we rolled into our respective beds.

The next day would be a quiet one, but Red Hart would resume our usual activities once Christmas faded with the new year.

And I needed a lawyer. The thought rose unbidden as I paused in the doorway, looking out past the boys to the stretch of land beyond the yard, covered in snow.

Our parents, Trav, and I needed to sit down with someone and go through the legal side of what the family wanted to happen to the ranch. It was a dark thing to think about at such a festive time, but the ranch was important.

Without it, we were still family, but the place brought everyone together and gave people who didn't have a home a place to put their efforts and their hearts.

My gaze shifted to Archer.

At least for the ones who were willing to stay.

Breath evacuated from my lungs. The ranch would be bare without him on it. For the first time, I experienced a pang of loneliness.

I joined the boys at the railing, listening to Jude's stories of Trav as a teen trying to tame a local bull — it had been a spectacular fail — and tried to enjoy what time the people of Red Hart were willing to give me.

"Anything I can do to help?" Simon's low, smooth voice, so different from Archer's, caressed the base of my neck.

I stood in my customary place in the kitchen, trying to work out the best way to carve up the turkey. It might be considered a formal dinner elsewhere, but for us, it was about getting food into the bellies of the men who worked the ranch for us.

The roasted bird sat in a huge dish, only just able to contain it. Crispy wings hung over the sides, and I batted more than one pair of hands away from it.

Simon's presence took me by surprise; I'd barely seen him throughout the day. Mom excused herself for the night early to a chorus of cheers in her direction as she climbed the stairs. I promised myself I'd check on them both after dinner.

His fingers grazed my waist, a small shock passing through my system at the contact. I twisted away with a half-smile, not wanting to make a scene but still unsure of myself. I stepped around the island bench, clutching a large bowl of buttered sprouts.

"Um, sure. Why don't you... take the roast in?"

I jerked my chin at the large bowl covered with one of my grandma's embroidered covers, circling around the island to get to the long table. Broad shoulders flexed beneath an almost indecently crisp, blue shirt as he lifted the heavy platter, muscles straining the material of his shirt sleeves.

Archer turned as I approached, sliding the plate from my hand and rearranging it on the table. Roasted meats mingled with Christmas spices and the underlying cranberry zing that seemed to permeate the house at this time of year.

Empty-handed, I fidgeted for a moment, then gripped the back of his chair for something to do.

"Is this what it's like... wherever you're from?" I asked. There was still so much about both these men I didn't know. While we'd always had an open-door policy at Christmas, we'd never had drifters come through so good at evading my questions either.

So determined to keep their secrets.

"It's warmer there." Archer turned, one corner of his mouth lifting. "Some years we get snow, some we don't."

"So, you're from the south," I blurted.

Simon looked up at me, curiously across the table, where he fussed with dressings for the roast.

Archer's fingers caught my chin, and I turned back to him with a start.

"Keep guessing, sweetheart," he murmured, but a twinkle in his eye told me he liked the challenge, and as much as I hated to admit it, I liked it, too.

The afternoon passed faster than I had expected. I cleaned plates from the table, checking the clock above the mantle with a small shock. It was after ten. The hands said their goodnights, one staying to drink with Jude while the rest peeled away to the bunkhouse. Simon cast a glance over his shoulder at me, turning back to comment on something the man next to him had said.

I finished up my own chores, kissing Mom's cheek as I checked on my parents in their room, but they were both asleep. Dad's pillbox sat near the edge of the table next to the bed. I almost knocked into it. Sliding it back, I noted its lightness. I'd have to go into town to fill his prescription again. I cleared up the few things from the day and slipped back downstairs without disturbing them.

Jude met me at the kitchen bench. He nudged my shoulder, nursing a beer. "Feeling any better? You were pretty out of it, cuddled up to Archer." He grinned, a familiar cheekiness shining in his eyes.

"I was sleeping on him," I corrected, heat flooding my cheeks as I realized what I'd said. "Wait– that's not what I meant."

"It's alright, Eve. He's a good man, yeah?" Jude shrugged. "He works hard, knows his shit. It'll be a challenge when he leaves with your brother away."

"Has he told you where he's from?" I asked, unable to stop the words tumbling from my lips.

Jude sent me a look. "You know better than to ask that."

I stared at my feet, still in their wooly socks.

"I know," I said softly.

"You know what?" Archer asked.

I looked up at his face, Jude already halfway across the room. He sent me a sharp grin over his shoulder. I shook my head. "Not half enough about you," I snapped, then covered my mouth. "I'm so sorry, you—"

"Earned that one." Archer supplied. He slid his hands in his pockets. "You don't know anything about me, Eve."

"I know who you are from what I see of you here."

"Which could well be an act." He tilted his head, his eyes fathomless as I lost myself in them for a moment. "I've only been here a week. Anyone could keep up a pretense that long."

"Is that what you're doing? You're actually a complete alphahole, and—"

"The billionaire sheik of an unnamed nation." Archer nodded. I giggled, rolling my eyes.

"Are you ever going to get tired of that?"

"No chance, girl."

I shivered, his eyes raking me, a small smile hinting at the corners of his lips. Tearing my eyes from his face, I looked around, but there were only a few of us left in the house. Jude and Simon talked quietly in the kitchen, and Kyle snuck out the door with an armload of food.

"Are you carrying on at the bunkhouse?" I asked, "Usually we keep going here."

"Maybe without your brother, they aren't as comfortable being rowdy."

I mulled over that for a moment. Archer poured me a glass of red wine. I took a sip, closing my eyes. "That's lovely. So, wait. Is it a bad thing they aren't comfortable here?" I came back to his comment from moments ago.

Archer shook his head. "Not at all. It just means they respect you too much to cross a few lines with you, to get too rowdy. It's a good thing for a woman running a ranch, pretty much on your own at this point."

"I have Mom, and I'd be lost without Jude," I protested. "We work as a team."

"Jude is their boss. He's not the owner," Archer said softly. "There's a difference."

I thought his words over, sipping my wine. Archer was right, but I'd never stopped to think about it that way before. I'd worked each day with everyone, organized food, and made sure the staff were happy and included. That they had comfortable sleeping areas and managed their pay.

It seemed the best way to keep reliable staff when you wanted them to work hard for you in sometimes-challenging conditions.

"I need to get my head around this stuff," I rubbed my hand over my face, smothering a yawn, "but not tonight. I want to check the herd before it gets too late or too cold. Especially after this morning. Thank you for taking the time to bring them in." Tears pricked the corners of my eyes. I ran both hands over my hair, sucking in a long breath.

"It needed to be done." Archer shrugged, watching me from the corner of his eye as he collected his jacket. "I'll come with you?"

I smiled. "That would be great."

Putting my glass on the bench, I told Jude what we were doing, and gave him a hug. "You know I'd be royally screwed without you. Right?"

Jude laughed at me. "Eve, you'd make this place run if you were the only person left on it. You're more formidable than you think. You just don't see it."

Shaking my head, I waved to Simon, packing things away in the pantry. "I'll lock up before I go to bed."

Jude nodded, turning away to answer something Archer had said. I smiled, watching the two of them laugh together. Archer *did* fit in well. The thought gave me a pang, and I grabbed my coat, not bothering with my hat or gloves. He could catch up to me when they were finished. Reasoning I'd only be out in the weather long enough to cross to the barn, I forwent the beanie and stuffed my feet into my boots.

I trotted across the yard. Snowflakes hung in the still air, ice kissing my cheeks as snow drifted over Red Hart. It had a chilled edge to it, and I wondered if we weren't in for a worse night than I expected. After the beauty of the day and our first snow last night, I'd expected the weather to close in faster, but we'd been blessed by a beautiful Christmas day.

I hoped our reprieve wasn't over.

I couldn't see any stars and got cold cheeks for my efforts. I opened the small, side door, slipping inside the warmth of the barn. The animals were in their pens — more than anything, I could smell them, dark as it was inside, and fumbled in my pocket for my phone and realized I'd left it in the house.

I debated checking the animals without it for a minute, but I couldn't see, and I didn't want to turn the big light on and startle them all.

My hand still wrapped around the door handle, I was surprised when it pulled outward. A dark shape stepped inside, the door closing to shut out all light.

I sighed. "Great. Archer? Or Jude. Have you got a phone? I can't see a thing."

I waited in the darkness, feeling more awkward by the second as the figure in front of me didn't answer. I stepped forward, straight into the person, and backed off in a hurry. Hard fingers closed around my waist.

A mouth nuzzled my neck. I shrieked, not caring about the animals any longer, pushing hard with my hands. I had no idea *who*, but I knew it wasn't Archer.

And right now, nothing else mattered.

"Get off me!" I yelled.

"But Eve, we worked so well together."

I tried to place the disembodied voice. "Simon?" I asked, twisting my hips from his grip and backing up as far as I could. "You shouldn't be in here. And you aren't to touch me again."

I began to circumnavigate the place I expected him to be, fumbling to find the wall in the pitch black that closed around me, and came up with nothing but air.

Where the hell is the door?

CHAPTER 14

"You looked so pretty tonight, talking about family." Simon's voice caressed my skin, sliding beneath my jacket. Blinded by the darkness winding itself around me, I wanted to throw up. A mix of revulsion and fear gripped my stomach, prickling my skin.

"You're drunk," I said firmly, ignoring my heart wrenching out of my chest with panic. My breath came in short bursts, and I tried to concentrate on slowing it while trying to find the door. Or the wall. Had I gotten turned around? The pervading darkness did nothing to help me.

Door. Must find the door.

"Come on, Eve." His hand scraped my sleeve. I bit back a scream. "I want to feel you against me."

My stomach lurched.

"Stop that," I snapped, letting my anger cover my fear, purely as I knew I'd freeze otherwise, and that was far less than helpful. My hand hit the barn wall. My breath puffed out in a quick exhale, with relief, this time. I edged sideways, fumbling for the handle. "This isn't appropriate."

"Appropriate?" He laughed harshly, his hand connecting with my waist as he swiped again. "Do you consider what you were doing with Archer that morning, *appropriate?*"

Yeah, you knew that was gonna bite you in the ass.

"Simon. Let's be clear." My hand found the door handle and turned it, or tried to. It jammed, unyielding under my grip. A painful shiver tore over my body. "I am not going to be involved with you at all. Don't touch me or kiss me again." To hell with manners. I wiggled the handle, and this time, it moved. "Are we clear?"

I pushed the door at the same time, skittering backward with the force of my movement as the thing finally gave.

Hands clenched around my waist. I swung wide, panting, my fear taking over. Apparently, I wasn't a freezer after all; perhaps more fight-and-run-away suited my style. The *oof* at my back stopped me.

"Archer?"

"You gotta stop hurting me, Eve."

I spun in his hands, wrapping my arms around his neck.

"Oh, thank God." I buried my face in the scent of him, desperate to get the touch of Simon off my skin, though barely anything had happened. Mostly pure luck, I knew. If I hadn't found the door if he'd managed to get his hands on me... I shivered, pressing my arms into myself.

"Eve, what happened? Where the hell is Haldon going?"

"He's gone?" I turned my cheek, not yet ready to step away from my safety barrier.

"Ran off. What the hell happened?" His cheek grazed mine, his chin tilting mine back until I stared into his eyes. "Tell me." Archer's voice was soft, soothing.

My lips pressed into a thin line, unsure I would be able to say anything. Then the words began to tumble out.

"He was drunk. I think. He kissed me. It's hellishly dark in there. The door wasn't where it should have been, and he kept trying to grab me. I couldn't find the door." The moment of panic revisited me, and my stomach clenched. Bile rose in my throat. "I'm not actually sure I can go back in there."

I frowned at the small doorway, babbling at him.

"He assaulted you?" Archer's voice was distant, his arms steel bands around my back.

I considered it. Something Dad had always said to me coming to mind too. *"If you're gonna accuse a man of something, make sure it's right and true. Could ruin his life. But always look after you first, Evie."*

Had he? He'd taken liberties but hadn't actually assaulted me. Well, mostly. Maybe I'd scared myself stupid for no reason.

"That's the most convoluted waffle I've heard in a long time. Did he touch you?"

"Did I say that out loud?" I asked, looking up at him.

Archer's lips pressed into a line, then he blew out a soft breath. "Yes. Did he touch you?" He repeated.

"Yes."

"Did he hurt you?"

"Well, no—"

"But, his attention wasn't wanted?"

"Hell no—"

277

"And you told him to fuck off?"

"No."

"No?"

"I politely told him I didn't want his attention, and I made it clear I didn't want him to touch me."

Archer snorted into my hair. "That's my girl."

"I'm what?"

Archer pulled me closer, kissing my forehead. "You want me to check the deer?"

"I don't want to stay out here alone," I whispered, hating how childish it sounded.

Archer shifted, leaning back. "JUDE!" he hollered.

Footsteps crunched over the already-icy ground. How long had I been out here?

Archer explained what had happened, asking him to check the deer for me. I sank into Archer's arms, not wanting to leave him.

"You should go to bed," he murmured, "I'll sort Haldon."

I looked up into his eyes, dark with a promise of violence, glad I wasn't on the other end of it.

"You guys can't kick him out tonight," I protested.

"He's sure as hell not staying!" Jude yelped, staring at me. "I'm sorry, Eve. He passed me on his way out. Made a joke, and I laughed at it, for fuck's sake. If I'd known..."

"It's not a big deal. Like he said, this is what happens when..." I dropped my arms, twisting my hands together.

"Eve." Archer's fingers tipped my chin back. "That's utter bullshit. The man can't be trusted, and he's not staying. Are you with me?"

"Yes," I whispered, completely unsure of myself. I shivered. His arms tightened around me.

"I'll look after him," Jude said firmly. "I've got a mind to lock him in somewhere and deal with him in the morning."

"I'm up for that," Archer said over my head, his voice edged with steel. "Right now, you're staying with me. Okay?" His dark eyes stared into mine, and I wouldn't have dared say no to him.

Mostly because I didn't want to.

"You okay with that, Eve?"

Jude, my champion.

I looked over my shoulder with a short nod, not trusting myself to speak, and sank closer into Archer. Jude's gaze traveled over us, hesitating on Archer's arms wrapped around me. I pressed deeper into his chest and held his gaze. He nodded, his mouth a thin line. I knew he read the coming heartbreak when Archer left, already resigning himself to weather it while my twin was out of action.

I didn't want to be alone. The coming hours before dawn lined up before me, promising terror at every shadow, knowing I'd jump at any sound at all, and I didn't want anyone else touching me.

Except for Archer.

He squeezed my shoulder, turning me in the direction of his cabin, murmuring something to Jude I couldn't hear or didn't listen to. I closed my eyes for a second, Simon's voice tearing around my head while I tried to escape him, fumbling for the door in the dark. My eyelids flung wide, little pants escaping my lips.

Archer's arm stayed wrapped around me the entire way, tucked tight into his shoulder. His frame might have been made of hardened metal, and though my eyes searched every dark space between us and his cabin, I knew I was safe with him.

Cold air brushed my face, but I lacked the energy to shiver beneath the wind's frosty fingers. Everything inside me was numb. I shook my head, trying to clear my thoughts, but they remained a muddled mess.

In my darkness, only one flame illuminated the shadows.

"Did I—" I started, but Archer cut me off before I could finish my thought.

"No, you didn't, Eve. Even if he'd started, then stopped when you objected, he still did the wrong thing. Drunkenness isn't an excuse for any sort of behavior like that." Archer's voice grated with years of experience.

I pressed closer to him. "Okay."

"You don't believe me?"

"Sort of?" My whisper, meant to be hopeful, came out as a pathetic, thin sound.

"Stop." Archer halted, turning me to face him. His hands cupped my cheeks, framing my face. I closed my eyes and leaned into him. "You are not at fault here."

"But if we hadn't—"

"If we hadn't, he would have obsessed over you, found you perfect, and still attempted it. Worse, in his mind, he'd have put you on a pedestal, and the only place to go from that high up is straight down. He'd blame you for something, and the end result would be the same. It's not your fault."

I swallowed the lump in my throat, and it finally sank to somewhere deep in my chest. "You seem to know a lot about him."

"I know people like him," Archer corrected, growling at me. He sighed, running a hand over my hair, smoothing it down my back. "Eve, listen—" He froze, turning in a semicircle either side of me, his grip tightening on my upper arms. "Let's go."

"Why are we going?"

"Because I don't want to be Christmas dinner for your local wildlife. Or anyone else."

Because what if Jude didn't find Simon?

I gripped Archer's hand, clamping my fingers around his tight enough to strangle a small creature. He didn't object, but we both powered through the fresh powder by an unspoken agreement.

I stretched my legs to keep up with Archer's longer stride, but the ache in my legs took my mind off what had just happened. The warmth of Archer's hand connected me to him like a lifeline, and I clung to it, desperately needing his thick cabin walls around us both.

And a bright light to ward away unwelcome nightmares.

Archer's cabin was a shadow between the trees at the end of the snow-covered path. I shoved my hair back from my face where it tangled, the damp strands stuck snowflakes melting to my skin, though I wasn't sure I had enough heat left in my body to melt *anything*.

Archer reached under the window frame for the key, never letting me go as he slid it into the lock. I stood in the shadow, pressed against the wall, just to feel something against my back. Open space suddenly seemed a threat it had never been before.

CHAPTER 15

"In," Archer urged, tugging me away from my safe spot. I slipped around him as he flicked the lights on, illuminating the entire room.

"You didn't have to bring me back here," I murmured, clasping my hands in front of me, trying not to fidget with my fingers.

"I wasn't sleeping with you in your bedroom, Eve. Your father might be incapacitated, but I don't think I'd stand up well to his rage.

"You saved me," I said reasonably. "He couldn't be angry about that. And, he knows, Archer."

He looked at me, surprise lighting his eyes. "You told him?"

I snorted. "Hell, no. He knew."

"Ah."

"Mmm," I agreed, the corners of my mouth twitching.

"Did you want to—" Archer's phone buzzed. He checked the screen, a smile growing over his face, and tossed it onto the counter. "Jude says it's sorted."

I closed my eyes, letting out a long exhale. "Thank God."

"Yeah. Coffee?"

"Do you want me to stay awake all night?"

"Right. Uh– whiskey?"

"You're on."

I took the small tumbler filled with golden liquid Archer offered, curling up on one end of the sofa. Archer set a fire with the remains of the firewood and sat at the other end, sliding his legs beneath mine.

"Are you going to be able to sleep tonight?" His eyes reflected the same auburn hues of his hair over the edge of his glass.

I shrugged. "I have no idea. I can try."

"Just don't snore when you do."

"I don't snore!" I protested, kicking his ankle lightly.

"You snored in the truck."

"Oh. Yeah." I bit my lip at the memory.

"What happened to you this morning?" Archer asked, turning his glass in his hand.

"What do you mean?"

"When you came downstairs, before lunch. You were pretty out of it."

"That's right. I fell asleep on you then, too."

"Is that normal for you?" His eyes held a small secret, and I had the feeling I'd have to dig for this one like I did all his others.

"Well, no," I considered, sipping my drink. It burned my throat but left gorgeous honey overtones dancing at the back of my tongue. "But it's been a stressful period, with everything that's happened this past couple of weeks. I guess I just crashed."

"I see."

I peered at him. "What do you see?"

"I see a woman who has plenty of energy and shouldn't have been affected by exhaustion like that when you had, what, done some admin work?"

"Newsletter."

"Right."

"You're gonna make me drag this out, aren't you? What do you think, Sherlock?"

Archer's head canted, and he drained his glass, spinning it between his hands.

"I think you were drugged." He said carefully, his eyes on me.

"No one up there spiked my drink," I joked, but his mouth didn't move at all. I frowned. "You're serious? Who? When?"

"Your teacup. I had an idea and tried the dregs in your cup. It tasted bitter."

I closed my eyes, trying to recall the morning. "I took the cups from the office and walked downstairs— yes, I drank what remained in the bottom."

"There was enough left for me to get a small taste."

"You stalked my teacup."

"Like I said, I had an idea. How you acted seemed out of character for you."

"Do you know me so well already?"

"I think I might. In some respects, anyway. I've seen how you deal with things under pressure. That covers a lot of bases in a person."

"Oh." I thought back on what he'd said. "Why would someone drug me? What did I drink?" He said nothing but waited. I sighed. "I'm too tired to work this out. Okay, it was bitter, and I slept. I got pretty vague, and I lost hours this afternoon. The day went really fast. But I've been feeling a crash-and-burn moment coming on for over a week now. Maybe it finally happened." I sighed, shaking my head as Archer watched me, waiting. I paused as the penny finally dropped into a very empty piggy bank. "Simon. You said he had opium."

"Yeah. Simon."

"Do you know him? Who is he, Archer? Who are you?" A massive shot in the dark. I had no idea, and admitting that to myself, hurt.

He smiled and huffed out a soft breath but didn't answer. I sipped my glass, watching him take his to the sink and wash it, placing it neatly in the drying rack. He wasn't going to answer my direct questions, but was there another way to get him to open up?

"That tastes incredible. Is it the one I put in here?"

Archer shook his head. "I brought it with me."

"From...?"

"I'm not dropping that now, after everything that's happened. If you want that one, Eve, you need to work harder for it." He laughed at me, but a tiny challenge lit his eyes.

"Mmhmm." I finished my drink and passed him the glass. My fingers brushed his, a jolt passing over them.

Archer stilled. "Bed?" he asked softly.

My eyes flew wide as I looked up at him. Everything about him stilled, coiled, waves of intensity pulsing from him, but the slightest curl of his mouth gave him away.

"Asshat," I grumbled while he laughed at me. My nose twitched. Well, I could give as good as I got.

While he washed up the glasses, I wandered to the bedroom door, curling my hand around the doorframe. My grip tightened enough to turn my knuckles white. I took a deep breath. Could I do this? My head stayed silent for once, and I took that as a good thing.

I waited until Archer's hands were free. I flicked my hair over my shoulder, looking back at him. "Coming?"

His eyes darkened, running over my body and back up. I forced myself to stand still. His gaze traveled to my hand, but I knew nothing in my posture suggested I was joking. I squeezed the door frame in a death grip, forcing my breath to even out.

His eyes flared in a minute movement as his inertia broke. He crossed the room in a few long strides, his arm snaking around my waist to pull me hard into his chest, his mouth crashing down on mine.

I gasped as his hands ran over me, squeezing, memorizing. His mouth moved hard over mine, demanding. Devouring. I tried to keep up with him, but I was swept away by the pure force of him. My hands curled around his neck, sliding into his hair. Cinnamon and whiskey surrounded me.

He drew back, leaving me panting in his arms. His eyes fathomless, every inch of me flared beneath his gaze as it left a searing path from my lips to my breasts.

"Eve, you don't have to do this. Not after what happened tonight."

"Don't stop this time."

"I won't." He paused, his brow dipping the tiniest amount. "Unless you want me to."

"No," I said softly but firmly. "I don't."

"Good." I read his eyes as they darkened to a treacle richness.

The only promise there was one of delectable sin.

"I want to, Rhys. Please."

It was the first time I'd used his name. I reached up, and his mouth met mine with a deep groan that sent a rush of heat straight through me, pooling at my core.

He tugged my shirt out of my jeans, sliding his hands up my bare back, flicking the clip on my bra open with one hand. His mouth left mine, traveling down my throat as he worked the buttons on my shirt.

I gasped as he pressed kisses along my neck, nipping at my collarbone. Sensation roiled through me, my breasts aching for his touch. My fingers trembled on the buttons of his shirt until it fell open. I slid my hands along the hardest muscles of his abs, defined and sculpted.

My shirt joined his on the floor. Archer ran his fingers under the straps of my bra, tugging them over my arms as he watched me. Heat flooded my face under his gaze, the tips of my nipples hardening into tight buds. He eased the material away, running his fingers along the sides of my breasts, grazing the soft flesh beneath.

I inhaled sharply, biting my lip. His hands slid around me as he lowered his mouth, his tongue tracing around the nipple but not actually touching it. Heat and desire melded between my thighs, and he'd barely touched me.

The rough pads of his fingers stroked my back as he switched from breast to breast, teasing. My hands wrapped around his arms, pressing into the hard muscle there, my head dropping back.

His hands dropped to my waist, running over my ass as his mouth returned to mine. I answered his kisses with a soft moan of protest. He smiled against my lips and tugged at the button on my jeans.

"Take these off."

I stepped back, slightly self-conscious beneath his darkened gaze as he watched me peel the dark denim away. My fingers hooked into the sides of my black lace panties, and I paused. Archer swallowed, his chest rising in a deep motion. I slid them down my legs and stepped out of the flimsy material, trying not to fidget as he looked me over.

He took a step closer, kissing me again. I reached for his belt buckle, but he knocked my hands away, kissing me hard. His hands ran from my shoulders to my ass, pulling me up harder against him. I whimpered with a building need, stretching up to link my hands behind his neck. His hands roamed over me, his tongue sliding between my lips to meet mine.

My hands drifted down his chest to the vee at his hips, tracing the edge of his jeans. I broke the kiss, watching him this time as I undid his belt, sliding the zipper down on his jeans. I traced the shape of him with gentle fingers, earning a groan between gritted teeth.

His hand curled into my hair, clenching tight as he pressed me down onto my knees. I pushed the stiff denim away, running my hands over him, brushing my open lips across the head of his cock. He clenched my hair tighter, pulling my head back to stare into my eyes as I played with him, stroking my hand the length of him.

He guided my mouth back to him, breath hissing between his teeth as I took him inside my mouth. His hand in my hair wasn't forceful but a controlled guidance, varying the speed of my movements as I traced my tongue around his cock.

He drew me back up to him, cupping my cheeks to kiss me deeply. I arched against his chest. He kicked his jeans away, lifting me onto his hips. The tip of his cock pressed against me, rubbing. Heat swarmed over me again as I wriggled, but Archer shook his head.

"Not yet, Eve," he murmured the words against my mouth, brushing his lips over mine.

He laid me back on the bed, letting my legs hang over the edge. I scrambled backward, but his hand caught my hip, halting my movement. Archer's eyes held mine, a promise swirling in their depths. A shiver coursed over me as he kissed me again, moving his naked chest down my body to tease my breasts again. I moaned as his mouth finally closed over one, sucking the tip between his lips, grazing it with his teeth.

My hands curled around his shoulders, tracing the hardened muscles beneath, pressing my palms flat against his shoulders as I arched beneath his teasing lips. Biting back a moan, I clung to him as he swept me up in the coiled energy that I knew he would unleash over both of us.

Archer pressed my legs open with his hands on my upper thighs, pressing back firmly as he stepped between them. His thumbs brushed the soft flesh there, spreading me bare before him. His fingers over me, stroking the sensitive flesh there drenched with my arousal and need.

I moaned, flushing hotter as he spread my own slickness over me, flicking his thumb against my clit. His mouth swapped the other side, nipping, teasing my nipple as he flicked my clit. Tiny noises came from my lips, my hips writhing beneath him, desperate for him to fill me.

He held me still, palming my stomach with one broad hand, flicking my clit again and again in the same rhythm he flicked my nipples with his tongue. I cried out, my orgasm smashing into me. Two fingers thrust deep into me. A scream ripped from my throat, my body arching and undulating as I curled around him. His mouth brushed mine, every nerve ending awake and pulsing wherever he touched my skin. My thighs clenched on his arms as wave after wave of pleasure obliviated me.

His arms wound around me, lifting me up the bed, cradling me to his chest, smattered with a fine covering of hair. I kissed every muscle there, nuzzling against his skin as aftershocks of pleasure turned me to liquid. He slid between my legs, leaving me for a second, then he returned. I blinked dozily at him, sitting back on his heels between my legs. My limbs felt heavy as he rolled a condom over the length of his cock, running his hand over himself a few times before he braced over me and kissed me deeply.

Dizzy, I whimpered, the tip of him against my swollen entrance. His legs braced against my thighs as his hand found my hip, and he eased slowly inside me. I wrapped my legs up and around his, my ankles crossing behind his back as I tilted my pelvis backward, drawing him deeper into me.

"Eve," he rasped against my mouth, "I—"

"If you promise me you're going to be gentle or slow, that's not going to work so well for me." I gasped as his hips shifted, and he thrust the last inch of himself deeper into me.

"Good," he growled. My gasp became a whimper as he moved again, and we found a rhythm together that covered us with sweat. Skin slid on skin, our breaths warming the other's flesh. The room and my world disappeared, narrowing into the dark eyes I lost myself in and the sensations rippling along my body. His arms tightened around me, sliding lower to lift my legs around his waist as he slammed us both back into the oblivion he taken me to before, his hoarse yells mingling with my own.

CHAPTER 16

Archer slumped over me, breathing hard into the curve of my shoulder. His fast breaths sent flutters of sensation across the spot, but I didn't move. I floated on the high of feeling him all around me.

He mumbled something into my neck.

I moved my head half an inch to look at him. "What was that?"

"Don't you move. I'll be right back."

My legs slid around his, coated in a fine sheen of sweat.

"You're not going anywhere." I snuggled back into him.

Archer laughed; a dark sound laced with pleasure that rippled along my spine. "I'll be a moment." He pressed a kiss to my lips, sliding from my embrace.

I sighed, curling onto my side, the feel of him still imprinted into my skin. He climbed back onto the bed, pulling me upright. I groaned in protest.

"Drink this, honey, then I'll get the lights."

I sipped water from the glass he offered obediently, sinking back into the pillows. The lights flicked off, shrouding the cabin in darkness, but fear no longer controlled me. Archer's arms wrapped around me, pulling me back against him. He drew the blankets over us, and I sank into a dream full of Christmas scents and the feel of his lips on my skin.

I rolled over, running into a bear-like warmth in my bed. Prying my eyes open in the early morning light, I came face to face with a pair of dark eyes. Archer's mouth curled at the corners as he pulled me into his arms, kissing me deeply. I pressed against him, first for warmth and to remember the feel of him from last night, then for something needier as my legs tangled with his, his knee sliding between my thighs. I whimpered against his mouth as he hardened against my stomach. Sliding between our freshly slicked bodies to wrap my hand around him, I mimicked the movement of his knee between my thighs.

Panting slightly from where his leg pressed hard against my clit, I pulled him closer, but he shook his head.

"Just a minute."

I groaned, flopping my head back onto the pillow. Archer laughed, picking his jeans up from the floor and pulled a condom out of his wallet. He tossed the small foil packet to me. I caught it, surprised my hands were operational.

"Would you?" he asked, leaning down to kiss me. I nodded, clutching the little packet as he helped me sit. My hands might be working, but my legs were in struggle town.

I crawled across the bed to him, his fingers catching my chin to tilt my head back. My back arched; I licked my lips as he rubbed the tip of his cock over my mouth, gripping my hair tight again. I slid my mouth over him, pressing my thighs together at his moan. His hand tightened in my hair, but he let me explore him, tracing the width and veins of him with my fingers and tongue. Eventually, he tugged my hair gently, drawing me back.

"Enough, Eve."

Flicking my tongue out over him one last time, looking at him. His fingers flexed in my hair, tugging my head back. I slid the condom on, running my fingers over him a few times, loving the way he filled my hand.

I pressed against his stomach, pushing him down, but he shook his head, slipping around behind me. He nudged me forward until I paused near the railing at the head of the bed. His hands circled my wrists, lifting them to the railing, curving my fingers around it.

"Don't let go," he murmured against my neck, running his fingertips along my arms.

He gently eased into me, sliding my hips away before he thrust inside me fully, then again. I mewled a protest, looking over my shoulder at him. His eyes were as dark as before. He pressed a hard kiss against my lips, his hands sliding from my hips to my breasts, tracing the shape of them with light fingers. I clenched with each caress, my nipples tight, aching for their turn.

I gripped the railing tight, shifting my hips against him, but he continued to tease me. My thighs were slick with my own fluids. He dropped one hand to brush lightly over my clit, sliding a little deeper into me. I shivered, gasping.

"Rhys, please—"

His fingers pinched my nipple and clit as he slammed inside me. I screamed, arching back against him. His arms wound around me, cradling me to his chest, my orgasm controlling my senses with him still buried deep inside me.

Archer held me tight within the bands of his arms, supporting me. I trembled around him, my head lolling back against his shoulder. His head dipped, his mouth meeting mine. Rough fingers dug into my hips, holding firm as he began to move within me again, his arm crossed tight across my chest.

My hips followed his, our movements matching. I pulled his bottom lip into my mouth. He moaned softly, his hand leaving my hip to curl around my stomach. I whimpered as he pulled me closer, sliding deeper. Our bodies moved harder together, against each other, until we collapsed, crying our pleasure against each other's skin.

I curled into his arms once we'd cleaned up. Archer threw a few small logs onto the fire, but the morning air decorated the inside of the windowpane with its icy fingers. He pulled the blankets around us, and I laid on his chest, listening to the rhythm of his heart, his hands stroking my hair.

The wind whistled around the cabin, the light of the morning darkening as the snow fell heavier outside.

"I don't think we'll be leaving here for a while," Archer pulled me across his chest, wrapping his arms tighter around me. "You should get some of that sleep you seem to be lacking."

"What about– about—" I pressed my lips against his chest, squeezing my eyes shut, but I couldn't get his name out. "I'm being silly."

"You're not. He's terrified the woman I—" He broke off, tapping the railing above us with his fist. "He'll have to wait a while longer. I'm not going out in this, and neither are you. Sleep."

"I'm not going to be able to sleep. I have to sort this out." I struggled to rise, propping myself up with arms that trembled where they pressed into the bed. The window outside showed only white. I couldn't even see the trees, and they were just outside. I pressed my face into the pillow. "Dammit."

"Honey, if you're not tired enough to sleep, I'll wear you out."

I raised my head to stare into Archer's eyes incredulously. "You can't be serious. My legs are still trembling."

"Only trembling?" he murmured, rolling me onto my back, kissing his way down my body despite my half-assed protests. "We can do better than that."

My hands curled around his shoulders as he showed me exactly how much my legs *could* shake.

By the time the snowfall thinned, it was well after the time I usually got out of bed. I peered out of the doorway. More than twenty inches had fallen in the last few hours, covering all of Red Hart in white. I grinned; the weather reports had been right. We should have stayed in the big house last night. But as Archer pulled his boots on, I knew I regretted nothing about the few hours I'd had with him.

I turned to look out over the tops of the trees. What little I could see of the house was almost completely snowed in from this side; the wind must have been blowing down the mountain. With snow banked to the top of the window frames at the back of the house. The track disappeared beneath a thick layer of snow; wet jeans would be inevitable by the time we reached the big house.

Archer slipped his knife in his pocket, followed by his phone, pulling the door shut behind us. "You ready?"

"There's a hot shower at the top of the stairs."

"Only if it hasn't frozen over."

"Well, there is that."

Together we launched off the stoop into the snow, sinking to our knees. The short walk back to the house became a long, icy trudge in freezing conditions. I gripped his hand tight, reveling in the few minutes we had left together, just us.

The tops of my thighs screamed with the heavy motion of lifting my legs above the snow, plunging them back down, and lifting the other.

Lift. Step. Slip. Repeat.

Even though I was fit, I was panting by the time we were halfway there. Archer looked at me with a glint in his eye. I held up my hand.

"Don't say it," I warned him.

He snorted. "You're no fun."

"That's not what you said last night."

He stopped, dark eyes assessing me. I swallowed beneath his gaze, memories of his hands and mouth on my body, crossing my vision. My face heated, melting snow that hit me instantly.

His hand slipped around my waist. "You're so damn beautiful."

Despite the snow coating both of us in a fine frost, he tipped my chin up and kissed me. For one last moment, I forgot the worries and sank back into him, a flaming beacon in the white-out that had become my world.

His arms around my waist, he helped me up the edge of the verandah, hauling himself under the railing. Archer's arm slipped around my waist in a one-armed hug, pressing a kiss to the top of my head. I leaned into him.

"Let's do this, huh?"

I nodded, my fingers clenching together. "I need to call my brother. I have to tell my parents. Oh, god. That will be..."

"You need to call the police. Or your local sheriff. Who is it?"

"Do you know the local sheriffs?" I asked, looking at him askance. "Been in many cells recently, Archer?"

"None I haven't escaped from." He winked while I gaped after him, unsure if he was kidding or not.

He held the door for me. I kicked off my boots in a hurry, shaking my jacket out and draping it over the drying rack near the door, heading for the stairs. Jude stopped me, standing where I hadn't noticed him sitting with Mom on one of the sofas. Her face was white, and she huddled into herself, not looking at me.

I turned back to Jude, who sported a purple bruise across his forehead. "What's wrong? And what happened to you?"

Jude's lips thinned in a hard line. I raised an eyebrow, and he blew out a long breath. "This

312

was Simon." He tapped his head with a wince, and I read the anger in his tone. "But Eve—listen, last night." He stopped. Just stopped talking.

There was a stillness about him I'd only ever seen once before when he'd been in absolute terror of a bull he'd tried to ride. It had tossed him, rushing at him while he completely froze. Travis had jumped the fence and bulldozed them both into the fence when the thing had charged. He'd never been so still.

Archer stepped up behind me, warmth radiating from him. "Talk, Jude."

His voice had a bite, and Jude reacted to it.

"Your father— Eve, he didn't wake up this morning."

I swallowed, trying to work out why he wouldn't wake up. Maybe too much whiskey? "You mean, he's unconscious?" I frowned. "Or in a coma? How did that happen? We can't get a helicopter out in this." I gestured to the white-out behind me.

Jude stared at me, mute.

Archer's hand slipped around my waist, squeezing gently. "Eve, I don't think that's what he means."

"What?" I turned my head to look up at him. Something stormy rolled behind that glinting dark gaze. I turned back to Jude, and it clunked into place.

My head emptied of everything in it, a void which refused to work. I tottered, the ground moving beneath my feet. Archer's hands tightened, and he pushed me gently into a lounge chair near Mom.

He nodded to Jude.

"Tell me what happened."

"I came in early. I couldn't remember if there was a lot of cleaning up to do after last night's fiasco. Plus, I needed some pain killers. Betty flitted about in the kitchen, but her movements were all disjointed. I spoke to her, but she didn't hear me. Then she looked up, clear as a bell, and told me your father was dead, and it was her fault."

I squawked, my gaze sliding to the couch where Mom curled into a ball. Archer shushed me. "Let him finish."

Pressing the heels of my hands to my eyes, I nodded for Jude to continue.

"I told her that couldn't be true and ran upstairs to check. I left her alone for a moment, and I thought she'd be okay. I'm sorry."

Bandages stuck out from beneath the arms of Mom's cardigan. "Did she—"

Jude scraped a hand over his head, ruffling his short hair. "She was right. I couldn't find a pulse or a heartbeat. I tried CPR, but I– it didn't work." His eyes were pleading into mine.

I blinked, the first tears swelling, and slid across the sofa to put my arms around him. The foreman who had been with us for the best part of fifteen years sobbed into my shoulder while my own tears fell silently.

"She didn't do anything to him," I said the words to myself in a broken voice.

"No, she didn't," Jude soothed me. "She's just blaming herself for an old man dying in his sleep." His own voice was rough with emotion.

"Thank you for trying," I whispered, our tears mingling.

Archer pulled out his phone. "I got your message last night," he said slowly, tossing it into the air and catching it again. He turned on his heel, staring at us. Jude straightened.

"I lost my phone in the snow last night, chasing Simon when he did this. Tree branch, I think."

I squeezed his arm, checking him over. Jude waved me away impatiently.

"So, you never sent me a message that said it was all sorted?"

Jude shook his head. "I never saw him again, after... I tried to get to you guys, but the snow started getting stupidly heavy. I honestly hoped the bastard would get caught out in it."

Archer stilled. Every inch of him stretched taut, a wire on a hair-trigger. "Is the house phone working?"

"Nah, I think it got knocked out last night. Means the phones are probably down, too."

"Not mine."

He flipped his phone again, walking up the stairs as he made a call. I looked over my shoulder, following him as he walked and slipped off the sofa to Mom, where she still huddled in her little ball.

"Mom?"

"I killed your father," she said before I could say anything.

"No, Mom, you didn't. You love Dad."

"His bottle of pills was empty. I must have used too many last night for his dose." She tightened her thin arms around her knees. I stroked her back, but she didn't seem to notice.

"You're always so careful with those," I protested, my mind trying to work logically while most of it had shut down. I registered the shock but still tried to function. *Focus on the living.* "Maybe he knocked the bottle over, or– or—" A horrible suspicion formed in my head, my heart wrenching for her as my brain began to turn over.

Mom started muttering to herself. I motioned Jude over as Archer walked slowly back down the stairs. Jude sat with Mom, talking softly to her. I rose, rubbing my throat where bile sat, tearing at my throat with acid. I could barely swallow past it.

"Rhys, I need to go and see him." I started, then stopped at the cold look in his eyes. It was like looking at a man I didn't recognize. I instantly regretted using his first name, a bitter reminder of the intimacy we'd shared throughout the night. "What is it?"

His lips pressed together until they turned white. "Your mother's teacup has that same bitter taste."

"What?"

"Eve, who benefits from this? What happens to the ranch?"

I stared at him, open-mouthed, trying to work it out, but my brain chugged slowly, thick with grief that hadn't fully developed yet.

"Uh, everything goes to Mom. She'd look after the ranch with Trav and I. Just, without Dad. I'd planned to get us all to a lawyer and sort out succession planning after the new year." My eyes stung, blurring my vision. Archer said something, and I blinked the tears away.

"Focus, Eve," he snapped. "What if something happened to your Mom?"

"Do I have to think about this right now?" I stared as tears tumbled over my cheeks.

"Yes."

"Fine. Okay. Well, it would be Trav and me. We would be the heirs to the ranch."

He nodded as if none of this was news to him. "And if Travis had an accident..."

"He did, though. Oh."

"And Simon came onto you last night, seemed to think you were made for each other."

I shuddered at the thought of the tall cowboy's hands on me. "We haven't found him yet. He could be anywhere."

"I've checked the house and the barn." Jude joined us, speaking quietly, though I noted he stood where he could still see Mom. I smiled at him with relief. At least one of us was thinking.

"Thanks, Jude. I told you we'd be lost without you." I gave him a watery mirage of a grin, the best I could manage before Archer turned my attention back to him.

"Eve, why do you care where Simon is?"

I blinked. "Because I don't want him anywhere near me again. God, he could be anywhere." I shivered again. "And aren't you suggesting he's got a hand in this somehow? It's like a stupid game of Clue."

"It depends on who benefits the most."

The detachment in his voice sickened me. "Okay, be a fucking asshole. I need to see my father." I pushed past him, but Archer caught my arm.

"Not yet."

Jude frowned, looking between us.

Archer nodded. "I spoke to your local sheriff. They'll come out as soon as they can with the coroner to investigate. With this weather, that could be half a day, maybe more. I'm going to look for Haldon. Don't go upstairs, and don't leave the house."

With a nod to Jude and a final look that sent ice through me, Archer turned away, his face no more than carved stone. The door banged behind him. I turned to Jude.

"What the hell just happened?"

Jude shook his head, open-mouthed. "If I didn't know better, Eve, I'd think he's just accused you of orchestrating all this."

I blinked twice before I lost my battle with the bile in my throat and made it to the kitchen sink. Vomit mixed with my tears as I threw the remains of my Christmas dinner back to where it came from.

CHAPTER 17

I sat with Mom, feeding her tea after I'd cleaned up the mess I'd made, as neither of us could stomach food. She barely spoke, staring into the fire, huddled on the sofa. Jude sat in Trav's recliner, only a few feet away. A chair he'd never touched before, but it was the closest he could come to us without actually being on the sofa.

Bless him, he seemed happy to give us the space Mom, and I needed.

By midday, Mom had fallen into an exhausted sleep. I covered her with a crochet rug and turned to Jude, my mind hyper awake as I thought things through.

"Do you believe what he said?" I asked softly, not sure if Jude would respond.

He shook his head. "No, Eve, I don't. He's out of his fucking mind if he believes it too. I think he was just going through everything he could to try to make sense of it."

"Is it possible Dad overdosed himself? Or had a turn during the night, worse than before? I know nothing about any of this sort of thing."

"Then, where did the pills go?" Jude asked, spreading his hands over his knees.

"They would have been all over the floor or the bed." I nodded, remembering how light the bottle had been in my hands when I'd shifted it on Dad's nightstand. Now, I wished I'd said something.

"Is it possible your Mom did actually give him too many tablets by accident? Not that I'm suggesting she did anything maliciously," he added in a hurry.

I waved his apology away. "It's fine; I've been thinking all those things too." I paused, unsure of how to go on. "But Archer also seemed to think that Simon might have something to do with this. And Travis' accident."

Jude leaned forward, propping his elbows on his knees. "He thinks Simon's in love with you."

"How—" I cleared my throat, bile rising again at his name. I cleared it with a painful cough. "How would that even work? He's only been here, what, a week, two weeks?" I scrubbed my head, but my brain turned to mush.

"They both have. And look what's happened. It's like, I don't know, an obsession."

I thought back on the accidents, the times Simon had made a pass at me, his words in the barn. I swallowed. "Okay, but Dad still had his turn before they both arrived."

"True. But no one can bring on a stroke, can they?"

I flung my hands in the air. "Jude, I have no idea. I'd just gotten used to the thought of Dad as he is, and now I can't even go see him."

"Fuck Archer, Eve." Jude winced at his own choice of words. "Go see him. He's your father, after all."

"I won't." I rose, clutching the teapot I'd repaired a few days ago. "Don't you get it? He's trying to work out if I've somehow murdered my father. If I go up there and– and touch anything, it'll tamper with whatever evidence there is if Simon *did* do something."

Jude nodded, his head dropping, and I knew he'd thought through at least as many possibilities as I had.

I curled back on the sofa with a fresh pot of tea I didn't pour, staring out at the snow that fell over the ranch, wondering what would happen to it. I wanted to call my brother, but my phone was upstairs in my room. Maybe. I tried to recall yesterday afternoon, but I drew a blank on the whole thing.

Hours lost.

I could remember giving Dad his present, sitting on the bed with him, and going through the pictures in the little album I'd printed out for him.

Mom stirred. I fixed her blanket, tears brimming again, but I swallowed them down, holding the grief back until I understood what was happening with my family. Waiting wasn't my finest skill, and though I knew I shouldn't bottle my grief, I felt the need to think it all through before Rhys Archer returned and accused me of something I hadn't done.

Jude got up after a few hours. "Snow's stopping. I'm going up to the bunkhouse to– to tell them what we know has happened," he said, stressing the word *know*. "Lock up behind me, okay?"

"Sure," I murmured. "I'm not going anywhere. I'll try to make something simple for dinner."

"You don't have to do that, Eve. We can fend for ourselves."

"It gives me something to do."

Jude nodded. "I get it."

I rose to hug him. "Thank you, Jude. You're more part of this family than you'll ever accept, but you are. Really. Thank you," I whispered. He nodded into my hair, wiping away tears of his own.

"I'm so sorry about your Mom."

"She's blamed herself, and I'm not sure what's going to heal that. Some answers, maybe." I looked at her. "At least she's sleeping now. That's a good thing."

Jude squeezed my arm. "You get some rest if you need to, as well."

"I can't. I'm too on edge waiting for whatever hell Archer is bringing back with him."

I pressed a hand to my stomach as it lurched.

"We got you, Eve. He's not going to take you off the ranch. I promise you that."

"Thanks," I whispered again. "Trav'd be proud of you."

Jude gave me a lopsided grin and grabbed his coat and boots, disappearing into the snow. It fell lighter, now, and I could see the barn and the trees beyond, glad the boys had put the herd away safely before the snow had really come down. But the thought of Archer as one of the *boys* prickled my skin. I wished I could erase the last two weeks, but then thought back on my moments with Dad yesterday, and I knew I wouldn't.

A shadow flickered by the barn. I peered into the snow, wondering if it was Jude or one of the hands, but surely, they'd have enough sense to stay out of the weather?

Another flash of movement, this time with color, and I recognized Simon's bright blue shirt, so new it easily stood out against the white covering everything.

He's no cowboy.

I should have known; those smooth hands had never worked a farm or burned callouses on a rope holding cattle or horses at bay. Had never done an hour of outside work.

There were no further flashes of color. My worry spiked for Jude, wandering about out there, and for Archer, looking for him. Even if he hated me for whatever he thought I'd done, I didn't want either of them to be surprised by Simon.

I slipped out the door, not bothering to grab my jacket, barely taking my eyes off the barn. Maybe he'd sheltered there after it had been checked? But surely Archer had checked it too? Unless... unless it was *him*, I shouldn't be trusting.

My head whirled with doubt; the moments in his arms this morning, the care he'd taken with me to the contrast of the stone-faced man, jumping from thought to thought faster than I could keep up.

I can't trust at least one of these men. Maybe both.

We'd let strangers onto the ranch, with my family the price for our openness. I swore we'd never let anyone else on it again without first being heavily vetted.

I edged to the end of the verandah, searching the trees and paths for Jude or Archer, but I couldn't see anyone. "Jude," I called softly, then a little louder, cursing my own stupidity when it echoed through the undergrowth.

My mouth clamped shut, I chanced a quick look back at the barn. Nothing moved. I sighed, wishing I'd stayed inside.

If I locked everything up and ran up to get my phone, surely that would be safer. Then I remembered Jude's comment about the phones and signal. The icy wind blew straight through my thin, long-sleeved t-shirt.

Wrapping my arms around myself, I wandered back to the door, but a sound beside the house drew me back where I'd come from. I revolved on my heel, my sock catching on the wooden boards.

A shadow passed my side. I twisted, trying to follow the shadow. Blue flashed across my field of vision, my eyes widening as a hand gripped my throat, cutting off my air in a brutal grip. I kicked, flailing, but he — *who* — *Simon?* — positioned himself behind me, and I couldn't reach back.

I threw elbows and feet at him, dropping and thrashing to loosen his hold but too fast, my vision sparkled with dots, my head dropping to my feet as I collapsed in a heap. Sharp pain in my back stole my breath, and I screamed soundlessly, the world wobbling around me.

Cold seeped into my side. I looked down, but I couldn't see anything, and the ranch disappeared.

Ice ran down my side, seeping into my skin until it couldn't feel any more.

And for that, I was grateful.

Every part of me that wasn't numb ached. I rolled onto my side, the world swaying around me. I blinked, tilting my head back, trying to breathe, but hardly any air came through my blocked nose. My mouth felt like paper. I chomped down and decided it actually was filled with paper.

A cold dread ran over me, though my soggy brain refused to acknowledge what it already knew.

My hands were frozen, the tips of my fingers numb, and I couldn't move them. The flash of blue hit my eyes from my memory. My stomach griped again, and I held back the urge to puke up nothing at all by determination alone.

My back ached in the center, winding around to my ribs with my heaving. Huffing as much as I could through my blocked nose, I fought the urge not to vomit, again and again, refusing to suffocate in my own spew. The paper seemed tied to my mouth. I blinked, my eyes focusing on nothing in the dim light. I rotated onto my other side. A white outline around a square window sat in the middle of my vision. I flopped around, and my head sank onto something soft. I inhaled as best I could, recognizing the odor instantly.

Archer, his own scent mingling with my own, where I'd slept with him last night. This morning.

I was in Archer's cabin.

God, had I got it all so wrong? Tears blurred my vision as the remnants of my family floated across my vision. The pain sharpened in my head and after a time, my eyes drooped closed against my will, and I fell into the darkness, surrounded by all things Archer.

I'd never felt less safe in my life.

"Wakey, wakey."

A dark square surrounded by the white lines burned into my vision; I would never be able to come into this cabin again. I swallowed dryly, my tongue sticking to the top of my mouth. It refused to budge, blocking my airflow. I flailed, tears running down my face as I snorted snot, swallowing on a throat that refused to work.

The paper disappeared from my mouth, icy water splashing into it. My tears mixed with the water, and I swallowed, grateful, and attempted to wipe my face on the sheets beneath me.

Hands gripped my arms gently and turned me. My stomach clenched tight, and I whimpered, not daring to open my eyes.

"Come on, sweetheart. Look this way."

My eyes opened, glad he'd spoken first. Knowing prepared me, gave me a sort of power to face what would come.

I rolled to face Simon, my hands biting painfully into my back, their bonds tearing the skin at my wrists. I didn't wince but took the pain as a sign I was still alive.

I planned to cling to that sensation for as long as I could.

His fingers reached out to stroke my skin, to touch me, after choking me, binding me, leaving me on a bed wet and covered in melting snow. I gathered my reasons and did exactly what Archer had suggested.

"Fuck *off*," I rasped, my throat raw from the gag-induced choking and what he'd done to me earlier.

His gentle smile disappeared, replaced with an ugly sneer. His eyes promised me pain. I glared into them and determined I wouldn't give in to whatever demands he wanted.

God, let him have demands.

"Is that the way to treat the man who loves you?" he asked mildly, his hands going to his belt. I tracked the movement with growing fear, but I knew he'd have a hell of a time getting my jeans off me. That would give me time to fight. I breathed, glad my brain was finally clear and working after the fog of the last twenty-four hours.

A fog he had induced.

"You choked me. You hurt me." My voice grated horribly in my own ears. "How is that treating someone in a loving way?"

"Mm, that's true." He nodded. "I should have taken more care. Here." He pressed a cup to my lips. The same one Archer had given to me after we'd been together. I swallowed hard, trying to get some of the fluid down. He took the glass away, staring down at me. "Not that he's got an idea who I am. Pathetic Ranger."

"Who?" I stared at him, not comprehending his words.

"Didn't you know?" Simon sneered, his lip curling to show teeth that appeared pointed in the dim light the old barn afforded. "Your precious Archer is a lawman. A Texas Ranger." He spat on the floor beside me, my head rolling.

Rhys? What?

"What?" I mumbled, tugging at the ropes that bound my wrists, but all it achieved was to make the skin rawer. Pain lanced along my arms, and I desisted.

Simon's mouth opened wider, those eyes I'd once found alluring now filling me with fear as he loomed over me, placing a hand on either side of my head.

"He's been hunting me for months now. I killed his boss after months of watching him. Watching Archer," he spat the name vehemently across the cabin. "He's so *loved*, your Ranger. Too loved. It's a joy to take something from him. Twice. I shot Sam Bernie, and the stupid bastard never got a look at me. Didn't know I'd been right here with him the whole time, while he hunted a ghost. And now his time is up. Idiot."

He dropped one hand to run his fingers across my jaw, catching it in a slow caress that sent shivers of revulsion rioting beneath my skin. He smiled as though I were reacting to his seduction, while all I wanted to do was hurl on him.

Rhys Archer is a Texas Ranger. He will find you.

I clung to the thought, but Simon's hands on me blinded my mind of him. Bile rose in my throat, and for a moment, I thought I would actually get a chance to do what I wished. Then his touch became harder, pressing his fingers into my skin, the muscles protesting beneath his onslaught, and my stomach tightened into a ball instead.

Long fingers wrapped around my throat, squeezing the same, swollen flesh there. He lifted me off the mattress with one hand to kiss me, his lips and teeth smashing against mine. I shrieked, thrashing at the intrusion, revulsion rising in me as his tongue invaded my mouth. I slammed my head from side to side, but he held tight. Dots appeared in front of my eyes, the world swimming again, or maybe it was me.

Snapping my teeth, I found nothing but air between them. Simon's hand closed around my throat again, squeezing hard. Panic prickled my skin, pain bursting over my skin in random places, my nervous system misfiring. He slapped me, hard, my jaw jamming shut with a clack as he dropped me back to the bed.

My mouth filled with blood.

Simon knelt on the bed, gripping my hair tight for a moment.

"I watched you last night, with him. Little slut, leaving the lights on and showing off to anyone who watched you. You'll be alright after you've suffered for that little sin." His touch gentled as I stared, a sharp metal tang filling my mouth.

My mind protested that it had been snowing like hell last night and the only person

I'd been showing myself to was a man I'd fallen in love with, but I only spat a mouthful of blood and saliva on the bed. Bright red pooled on the white sheets.

He stroked my cheek once, then stuffed material into my mouth, tying it behind my head. I stared up at him, willing my terror not to show through as I inhaled through my nose, making the breaths as even as I could.

His lip curled as he rose, towering over me, the belt folded neatly in his hands. He dropped one end. It unraveled, coiling on the mattress in an uneven heap — his smile as dead as his eyes as he rolled me onto my front.

"Scream into the pillow, love. It will help with the first few strokes."

The belt snapped across the backs of my arms, the tip digging into my shoulder blades. I sobbed into the pillow, trying to breathe as it fell again and again.

He stopped, eventually.

My body ceased feeling as I retreated into a corner of my mind, reliving every touch, every moment I'd had with Rhys.

The outcrop, discovering the Christmas scent of him. That would be my memory.

Him pouring a small fortune of sapphires into my hand, giving me his trust.

Promising we'd make memories together. And we had.

Somewhere above me, people were shouting. Simon must be angry. I closed my eyes and dived back into my memories.

I emerged into a dream with Archer's face right above me, his breath tickling my ear. I wiggled, half laughing, though the sound wasn't what I expected.

"I've always loved your hair," I rasped, running my fingers through it. My shoulders ached, but I ignored them for a moment. "It's got these beautiful red highlights. I saw them on the first day at Beanie's." My throat started to ache as he lifted me in his arms.

The ache moved to my back, where it became a burn, stripping the skin raw. I gritted my teeth as tears ran down my face. At this rate, I'd need an IV of salt to keep going. A small giggle escaped my lips that became a cough, lancing pain through my neck and shoulders. That only reminded me of Dad, a waterfall cascading over my cheeks in a salted mix of grief and terror.

I pushed the pain back with the rest of my issues, focusing on Archer's face.

"Come on, honey. Let's get you somewhere warm."

My brow dipped; this wasn't in my memories. But it sounded good, so I went with it. "Where are we going?"

"Somewhere safe." His head dipped, his mouth brushing mine in a gentle kiss that made every inch of me shiver.

"That sounds good," I said, shivering again. And again. I pressed into his arms. "Why am I cold? You're so warm."

"She's in shock!" Archer called over my head. I stared up at his silhouette in something like awe. Ranger. Texas Ranger. The sun must have broken through the snow clouds, casting him in faint relief.

Sound merged with memory in confusion that overwhelmed my senses. I tried to raise myself against him, but nothing worked.

"Where's Simon?" I asked, trying to look around, but that hurt, too. "You're real, aren't you?"

"As real as I get, honey. Simon is rocking a broken jaw." Archer flexed his fingers beneath me.

I smiled. "I took your advice."

"What was that?"

"I told him to fuck off."

Archer laughed, pressing a kiss to my head. "That's my girl."

His words lit something warm in the void of my heart, and I knew it would heal. Sometime.

"Ranger. That's what he called you."

He huffed into my hair. "He said that huh?"

Arms gathered me, putting me on a soft bed, but that took me away from Archer. "Wait. Please," I called, my heart breaking as he stopped walking, doors closing between us.

My heart shattered a little as the engine started, the vehicle rumbling beneath me, and somewhere in my head, I knew this memory was more real than the others.

A bang stopped everything, my back wrenching on the soft bed. Without Archer, the pain returned in full. Something snapped near me, and I cried out, searching for Simon, but only two men in puffer jackets were in the ambulance with me.

The men chattered at each other, hooking me up to machines. I batted at their hands, staring at the door, willing it open. I figured if I pushed hard enough in this half-reality, I'd get what I wanted.

Miraculously, it worked.

A thin slice of light grew between the two doors, Archer slipping between them and slammed them shut with a bang.

The two paramedics froze, turning together to stare at him.

He raised his hands, palms up.

"He's like that," I apologized for him in my sandpaper voice. "Bull in a china shop. He really can't help it."

One of the paramedics snuffed out a laugh behind his hand, the other shaking his head sadly. Archer slid up the stretcher to squat beside me as the ambulance rumbled to life again, trundling down the drive to Red Hart Ranch.

"Thanks," he murmured, leaning in to kiss me lightly, "how are you doing?"

Oh, tortured by an obsessed madman, half-choked to death and frozen in the bed we'd had sex in while I doubted you.

A single tear slid down my cheek, an improvement from the usual cascade.

"I'm fine," I whispered. "Where's Simon?"

"Haldon is—" Archer hesitated, sliding a hand over his hair. "He's on his way back to Texas. My deputy will help me hound him there to answer for the death of Sam Bernie."

"Your friend." I frowned, trying to remember. "Why Texas? Why not here?"

Archer gave me a half-smile that didn't reach his eyes. "If he's arrested here, he answers to Montana state laws. If he's arrested in Texas... I know that system pretty well. I want him convicted there."

I was quiet for a moment. "So, he won't be arrested here."

"No."

"But, you'll chase him back to your home." I struggled with the idea. "That's why you knew you had to leave. All the time, this is why you can't stay."

Archer nodded slowly. "I should have been there for Sam. I have to make this right."

"Simon mentioned him. Your friend." My croak withered into nothingness at the end of the word.

Archer pressed his finger over my lips. "Let me talk. Save this," he stroked my neck with a gentle touch, "for phone conversations." I tilted my head, studying his face. He smiled, his eyes creasing as he drank me in, answering the question I couldn't ask. "If I can herd Haldon back to Texas, he'll be convicted for murder... amongst other things. I have to get him behind my state lines to do that. He killed the man who brought me into the Rangers, who mentored me for the last twelve years. Sam was like an extra father. I need to put this to rest, however long it takes. But I want to come back to you afterward. Can I do that? Will you wait?"

Would I wait for the man I'd envisioned loving me while a man who professed to love me whipped me? I nodded as emphatically as the neck brace the paramedic fitted around my throat allowed.

"Yes," I rasped, the tears falling anew. "If you go, please come back."

Please. Please don't leave me.

His eyes glittered. "I'll come back to you. I promise."

Archer left me at the paramedic's station. His hands tangled with mine throughout the trip. But about halfway to the nearest hospital, some four hours away, the painkillers kicked in. Fun for me, but probably not so much for the rest of the occupants crowded into the ambulance.

Never-the-less, Archer didn't let go of my hand the entire trip, his fingers tangled firmly in mine, a testament to the promise he'd made.

And despite the excellent drugs delivered to ease my suffering, I believed him.

My wounds were somewhat superficial. Archer said the skin on my back probably wouldn't scar; my arms and hands had taken the brunt of Simon's anger. I had a suspected wrist break, but my fingers, while swollen, appeared to be fine.

The backs of my arms were flayed to small strips.

One of the paramedics muttered about skin grafts. I tried to follow his movements, but the neck brace restricted me from doing pretty much anything other than stare at the ceiling. Archer moved while the man put dressings on my arms, sliding another drip into my other hand.

"I feel like a Terminator with all this stuff sticking out of me," I whispered to Archer, where he sat, stroking my feet through thick and decidedly-unsexy socks.

"You'll be fine, honey. You're so much tougher than all of this." He leaned forward, looking into my eyes before the paramedic shooed him back.

This seemed to be the general term we were using to cover everything that had happened at Red Hart over Christmas. It had been a hell of a year, but Archer was right. I *could* come back from this, and I would. As would the ranch. Even without Dad there, we'd chug along and remember him even more for it. I thought of the photobook I'd made for him, and the tears flowed anew.

Archer excused himself to speak to the medics.

It gave me a moment to reflect, though I knew I would have plenty of time when he left to do...whatever a Texas Ranger did. I had no idea and decided googling that would keep my mind off things once I got to the hospital.

Archer squatted back where he had been before, but I couldn't turn my head to look at him; I just listened.

"We're almost there." I gripped his hand as tight as my arm would allow but refused to let him go in any case. "They'll treat you, get you sorted, and then you'll get a shared room. With your brother."

This time I did turn my head, despite the discomfort and the squawking medic in my ear. I grinned at Archer. "Did you do that? Thank you," I wheezed at his nod as my head was straightened, and I got to fixate on the ceiling of the ambulance again.

"Jude has my number. He's going to put it in your phone. You're not going to get rid of me that easily," he warned, stroking my wrist with his thumb. I lay silent, thinking. He tugged on my hand. "Eve?"

"Are you going to want me after what happened with Simon? And D-dad?" I asked, resembling a human waterfall.

He'll be gone soon — just one more loss in a long line.

Archer hovered over me, batting away hands flapping at him.

"I will come back to you, no matter what that bastard did, Eve. I'm coming back. For you. Not the ranch, not the mountain. Though it's pretty, I'll admit. But none of it means anything without you there with it."

The medic coughed.

I ignored him. Archer's mouth twitched.

"Besides, who's gonna keep you out of trouble with Black Hill?"

My eyes widened. "Oh, my God. Pierce will be a nightmare. Did you have to remind me of that?" Archer's grin was my only answer. "Quick, though, what's happening with Dad?"

His face sobered. "It'll go to Coroner's Court, with your mother's permission, then I'll put a case together with the evidence, and he's looked after according to his will. Please do tell me he has one?"

I nodded. "It's with the family lawyer in White Cap. And there's a copy with all the paperwork in the safe."

Archer visibly relaxed. "Good. Call me if there's trouble, and I'll do everything I can to get back to you as fast as possible."

"But your job. That's... kinda location-specific. What will you—"

"I've spoken to customs. Part of my job is regulating what comes across the border between Texas and Mexico. Cartels are a big problem with drugs there, the same as people trafficking and rustling. Actually, it appears we've had an issue with one of my men this Christmas with cattle. Overstepped the mark a bit, but it appears to have turned out alright. He didn't step on too many toes."

"So, you... organize a group of Rangers?"

Archer gave me a wry grin. "I'm the Captain of the special ops division. Chasing a murderer across the country, crossing state lines was overstepping *my* bounds, so I can't be too hard on a man in my unit who did something similar to save a life. I'll answer to that back home."

"You saved my life," I said softly. "If you hadn't chased him, I—"

"You probably would never have heard of him. He pushed this far because he knew he had a tail."

"Wouldn't he have done that to anyone? I mean, regular police and sheriffs would have pursued him too."

Archer shrugged, his face darkening. "Perhaps."

"Archer. He's a psychopath. Please, do me and everyone else a favor and find him, take him away from places like Red Hart. Can you imagine him doing this somewhere else?"

"All too well."

"Well then. Catch your asshole and get *your* ass back to me."

Archer peered at me. "Good drugs?"

"The best."

The ambulance stopped, the medics gratefully abandoning us for a moment. Archer leaned down, kissing me gently. I closed my eyes, breathing him in.

"Stay."

"You know I can't."

"But, you want to?" I opened my eyes as he drew back.

"Hell, yes, woman, I want to." His eyes darkened, and he stroked my face. I held back tears, but I knew he saw them.

His head dipped, he kissed me sweetly, gently. I strained against the brace, but his hands on my cheeks pressed me back.

I love you.

The words were on the edge of my lips, but I couldn't say them. I gripped his hand tighter. "Come back."

"Ranger's promise."

EPILOGUE

I ran my fingers around the deer's hindquarters. She pressed to my side, quivering. Her teats still protruded. She hadn't yet adjusted to the loss of her young. I pressed my hands gently over her side. The loss of her fawn had quietened her; her wounds inside still open, rather like mine. My arms hadn't required grafts after all and were healing faster than the doctors expected.

Having Trav and me in the same room turned out to be a terrible idea. We were the rowdiest pair in the ward, and we only got worse when Rachel and Jude turned up to stay overnight while the nurses sorted our release.

One movie night, several trundle beds, and a bucket of popcorn, which mostly got thrown at the television later, we'd been yelled at by several irate nurses. Thankfully, we got a shift change in the middle.

Being with my twin made my losses easier to cope with. We even got a room psychologist who talked us through what we needed. She overstayed her welcome with my brother when Rachel turned up and saw her flirting.

That moved her on rather fast.

Dad's funeral was held in our absence, though we were able to attend via a video uplink. Tears flowed, and we shared as many memories of him as we could.

Jude looked after Mom until we returned. Although getting back to the ranch managed to be an arduous journey for both Trav and me, being home made all the difference to our recovery.

Red Hart's recovery.

"Eve!" Jude yelled across the yard.

The deer started. I shushed her, keeping the rhythm of my hand steady.

"What is it?" I called softly over my shoulder.

"You need to see this!" Jude yelled again. I continued my shushing, unsure if I was calming the deer or me. Perhaps a bit of both. "Look! I– oh, shit. Sorry," Jude whispered, his large frame dwarfing me.

I rolled my eyes. "That's a bit of a contrast," I reproved him.

Jude shrugged. "Yeah, well. I thought you might want to see this."

He shifted, and I noticed the bundle in his arms, puffing his jacket out. The cloth jerked, what looked like an old work shirt of his, and a soft, tan-colored head poked out.

My mouth dried. "Where did you find her? Him?" I looked up at the foreman as he slid the bundle into my arms, zipping his jacket up.

"Out near that copse in the backfield. The deer we lost yesterday? I think this might have been her offspring. She was pregnant, but he was so little, and we were so distracted that we didn't notice. This little guy came early. Boy." He grinned, Jude's blue eyes bright as I plucked at the material, but the hooves got tangled, and I desisted.

"Have you named him?" I asked as the creature nuzzled my shirt. "He's hungry. Do you think—" I bit my lip as the reason Jude was showing me the fawn fully hit home. He nodded, reaching out for the mother. She stamped a hoof nervously in the smattering of snow still covering the ground.

I held the bundle out to her. She sniffed the head of the fawn, her ears laid back, and I lowered it slowly to the ground, tugging the wrappings away. It found its own feet, thin legs quivering as it nuzzled at the teats on offer.

My breath caught as I prayed the mother's milk would let down.

The deer huffed softly, the tiny mouth latching on. It sucked for a moment, but nothing seemed to be coming out. A whine came from the starving fawn's mouth, a pitiful plea of loss and desperation.

"I'll get a bottle—" I started, but Jude nudged me.

Milk pulsed around the fawn's mouth, the stopped-flow of milk from the mother's loss quickly becoming a waterfall. Jude's arm wrapped around my shoulders in a one-armed hug. My lips stretched in a wide smile as tears glazed my eyes.

"There's always something incredible in the world," Jude murmured, squeezing my shoulder.

I snapped a few pictures to send to my brother, and my phone vibrated in my hand as a message came through. I jumped, nearly dropping the thing. I opened the app, wondering what Trav wanted and muttering to myself about twin-timing, but my brother's name didn't flash up on the screen.

Archer: We caught Simon. I'm coming back
     to you.

Tears glazed my eyes, and for the first time in weeks, they were of joy.

Rhys Archer was coming back.

I smiled, squeezing out from under Jude's arm to crouch beside the tiny miracle that would heal the grieving mother's heart.

Miracles *did* happen.

Rhys was coming back.

ARCHER AND EVE
WILL RETURN IN:
MISTLETOE ON THE RANGE.

FOLLOW ARCHER AND EVE
IN THEIR OWN SERIES,
RED HART RANCH
and
TEXAN DEVILS.

READ ON FOR RED HART
RANCH RECIPES

AND AN EXCERPT OF

BLUE BLOODED BROTHERS

BOOK I

COLLISION

The recipes used at Eve's Christmas table were donated by readers (though Simon's baked ham is my own recipe). Each Red Hart Ranch book will have its own food, and I'd loved to include the comfort foods you love (especially if you're willing to share your own recipes in print!). Call outs will be my newsletter.

You can sign up here:
https://BookHip.com/CNMQFX

CAGE'S MOM'S GUMBO

Recipe for the chicken, sausage, and shrimp gumbo:

1-2lbs of chicken

1lb of small shrimp

1lb of andouille or smoked sausage

1 bag of okra

1 1/2 white or yellow onion diced

2 stocks of celery diced

2 green bell pepper diced

4 cloves of garlic sliced thin

1 cup of flour

SEASONINGS TO TASTE:
Tony Chachere's
Seasonal
Garlic powder
Onion powder
Black pepper
2-4 bay leaves
File
Rosemary
Parsley
Sage
Oregano
Cayenne
Dice up your onions, bell peppers, celery, &
garlic

Take your cup of flour and place it in a
skillet. Turn the stove on medium-high, do not
step away; it's very important that you don't
step away. Whisk the flour till it's almost black,
don't worry, you want it like this.

It's going to take a while but be patient.
Once it is a deep chocolate/black color, add
water or chicken stock. It gets thick but keep

stirring and add more water until it thins out. Turn off the heat.

Get a stock pot or a deep pot out. Place your diced up vegetables in there with a touch of oil. Turn the fire on to medium-high to cook the vegetables, just a touch. I would say a minute or two. Then add your roux, add more water or stock as needed.

Cook until vegetables have broken down. 30 minutes to an hour. Make sure you cover it; it will help cook them faster. When they have cooled down, add your seasonings to your taste. Place the cover back down and cook for 10 or so minutes.

Cut the chicken into bite-size pieces and season it to taste. Add the chicken in and cook until it's fully cooked, covered.

Cut the andouille or smoked sausage. Add it in and cook for about 20-30 minutes, covered.

Add the bag of okra and bag of shrimp and cook until the okra isn't a vibrant green and has broken down some. Leave the cover off at this point.

Serve over rice.

A SHY DRIFTER'S CONTRIBUTION TO THE TABLE

2 cans of green beans

2 cans of Cream of mushroom soup

Add fried onions as topping

You mix the beans and soup together and bake in the oven for 30 minutes at 350F. Warm it thru, then top with the onions. It's one of my favorite dishes and really simple 😁

SIMON'S DINNER CONTRIBUTION TO EVE'S TABLE

Large leg of ham. Triple smoked is fine, as long as it fits in your oven!

1 pkt glazed or glace cherries

Cloves for decoration

Toothpicks

Glaze:

3 oranges, juiced. Pips can be squashed in as well, and you might be able to use the rind in a salad or dressing.

3 tbsp honey or treacle.

2 tbsp maple syrup (optional)

2 tsp mustard (I use dijon, pick your favourite flavour)

2 cups brown rum - we use Bundaberg Rum or
Spiced Captain Morgan's

1 tsp All Spice

1 tsp Cinnamon

Mix well.

Preheat to a moderate oven at 350F. Score inch square diamonds with a freshly sharpened knife. If you go quite deep in the centre you'll end up with large chunks of baked ham people will cut off and eat until they are stuffed. Place in baking tray and glaze ham with a light brushing (Wide basting brush works well).

Place ham in oven. Baste every 20-30 mins, turning the ham hourly. Depending on the size of the ham, this could be 90 mins - 3 hours. If you've made deep cuts, the ham will start to open up. Glaze between the cuts for extra flavour as it caramelises. Continue glazing and turning as needed.

When ham is ready, remove from oven and decorate with alternate glace cherries on toothpicks and cloves or just cloves or cherries to your preference. Can be served with salad, roast vegetables, and candied orange slices.

CONTRIBUTED BY JODI RAYNES

BROUGHT TO THE TABLE BY KYLE

Beat 4 eggs, 1/4 cup white sugar, 1/4 cup vegetable oil, and vanilla extract together in a bowl; stir in baking powder. Slowly stir flour, about 1 tablespoon at a time, into egg mixture until a soft dough forms. Roll dough into small balls.

Heat 2 cups vegetable oil in a large saucepan to 350 degrees F (175 degrees C) or until you see little waves on the bottom of the saucepan.

Working in small batches, fry dough balls in the hot oil until lightly browned, 2 to 3 minutes per batch. Transfer struffoli to a paper towel-lined plate using a slotted spoon.

Heat honey in a saucepan over medium-low heat. Slowly mix 1/2 cup sugar, a few tablespoons at a time, into honey until sugar is melted and glaze is smooth, about 5 minutes.

Transfer struffoli to a large bowl and pour glaze over the top; toss quickly to evenly coat before glaze hardens.

Form struffoli into a tower-shape or Christmas tree-shape on a serving plate. Sprinkle nonpareils sprinkles over the struffoli.

SIMON'S DESSERT

1 can of pumpkin puree

1 package of cream cheese

2 containers of cool whip

A graham cracker crust

1 TBS of pumpkin pie seasoning

1 cup of sugar

1Tps of vanilla extract

1 box of vanilla pudding

Mix one container of cool whip, cream cheese, and sugar together. Put in bottom of crust. Then mix pudding, pumpkin puree, pumpkin seasoning and vanilla together. Put on top of bottom layer. Then put cool whip as topping if wanted 😊

YIELD: 1 8- OR 9-INCH CRUST

MIX AND PRESS IN PIE PAN:

1 package graham crackers (1/3 pound), crushed fine or 1 1/4 cups fine graham-cracker crumbs

1/4 cup sugar

1/4 cup margarine, melted

Bake about 8 minutes at 350 degrees or until edges are as brown as desired; let cool. For an unbaked crust, chill 45 minutes; fill. Great with chocolate pudding or as Baked Alaska base!

EVE'S CHRISTMAS CONTRIBUTION

The following Chocolate Meringue Pie has a rich chocolate taste. Note that this recipe does not call for sugar or margarine.

Carol's Favorite Flaky Pie Crust (above)

Yield: 2 single-crust pie shells

2 cups sifted regular flour

1 teaspoon salt

3/4 cup Crisco solid shortening

1/4 cup water

Preheat oven to 450F degrees. Sift flour before measuring; spoon lightly into measuring cup and level without shaking or packing down. Combine flour and salt. With two knives, cut in

Crisco until uniform; mixture should be fairly coarse. Sprinkle with water, a tablespoon at a time; toss with a fork. Work dough into a firm ball with your hands. Divide dough into two parts and press into flat circles with smooth edges. *On a lightly floured surface, roll one crust to a circle about 1 1/2 inches larger than inverted pie plate. Gently ease dough into pie plate. Trim 1/2 to 1 inch beyond edge; fold under and flute edge by pressing dough with forefinger against wedge made of finger and thumb of other hand. Prick bottom and sides well with fork. Repeat* with second crust. Bake both crusts at 450 degrees for 10 to 12 minutes or till golden.

A NOTE FROM THE AUTHOR

Thank you so much for reading all the way through Eve and Archer's first Christmas story. I do hope you love them and Red Hart Ranch — there will be plenty more stories set here and I'd love to share them with you. I'd also really love it if you could take the time to leave a review on Amazon. Reviews really do help both authors and readers in choosing a book and knowing what you love and want more of! Please do consider leaving a review for SNOW ON THE RANGE and you'll have one very appreciative author.

ACKNOWLEDGEMENTS

Red Hart Ranch has been one amazing ride! Thank you for reading Eve and Archer's story — they *definitely* get their HEA (they really have worked for it already), and I promise it will be another Christmas story worth waiting for.

Montana is difficult to see from Downunder, but Lila Grey and Ashely gave me such wonderful insights into the amazing landscape to make Red Hart Ranch real. Plus, add in that cover from JS Designs, and I had my inspiration! Any mistakes are mine alone, but my desire to visit those remote and amazing borderlands in person grows daily.

Because this book is set in the US, unlike my other books, i took the time to write this in US english, and learn some local slang — thanks to Ashley again for picking out all my Aussie words that slipped in there!

My editor, critique partners, and ARC team — you all do such an amazing job. Plus, all my writerly friends who have spent the year hearing me bang on about RHR and its occupants. Your patience is greatly appreciated! Thank you for allowing me to fill the air with snow and cinnamon regardless of the season.

Thank you to all the amazing readers who contributed to Eve's Christmas table! I was so excited to be able to use your holiday favourites! It's really made this book so special for me. And I might be making some myself this year.

My amazing husband and kids manage to survive while I write, and my 7-year-old daughter sits with me to write, too, every week, cooing over new book covers and book swag.

Being able to share my love of stories to escape into keeps me going through the hardest chapters. I cannot say how grateful I am for you all, so I'll give you hugs instead.

Tony, thanks for the coffee refills.

And you. Thank you so, so much for reading all the way through book 1 of Snow on the Range. I hope you loved it and fell into a very special Montana Christmas, and I can't wait to share the stories of all Red Hart Ranch's family with you. Archer will return to Red Hart. I promise.

Sofia xx

ABOUT THE AUTHOR

Sofia is a romantic suspense author from Brisbane, Australia. She started writing romance when she couldn't find the books she wanted on the shelves in her local bookstore and became addicted to storytelling. She exists on a diet of coffee and champagne and routinely kills her collection of tortured orchids.

www.sofiaaves.com

Join Sofia's newsletter & get a free Blue Blooded Brothers short story:

https://BookHip.com/CNMQFX

BLUE BLOODED BROTHERS

COLLISION

book 1

www.books2read.com/Collision-LQP

BLINDSIDED

book 2

www.books2read.com/Blindsided-BBB2

SENTINEL

book 3

www.books2read.com/Sentinel-BBB3

IMPACT

book 4

www.books2read.com/BBB4

RECKONING

book 5

Coming 2021

SERIES SHORT STORIES

POLITICS & PAPERWORK

www.books2read.com/Politics&Paperwork

BREACH OF DUTY

www.books2read.com/BreachofDuty

DARK REFLECTIONS

Logan's story.

Coming Soon.

READ ON FOR THE FIRST
CHAPTER OF CAL AND
MILA'S STORY IN

COLLISION

BLUE BLOODED BROTHERS BOOK 1...

CHAPTER ONE

MILA

Tiny feet pattered the worn carpet, glitter coating it with false splendour. The little girl wended her way between patrons. Some were blessed with stars, some with promises of happiness and love; others became apples and bananas. Too much *Ben and Holly*, I recalled from when I'd been forced to babysit for my best friend.

I tried not to look over to my left, the red shoe that– I spun away, and refocused on my task. The man behind me shuffled his feet. I flinched as he dug the pistol into the small of my back, and shivered, my skin prickling.

The small office of Central Bank was being held up, and no one outside had noticed. Business operated as usual in the main street through the broad, glassed front as it did every day.

"Oooh, sweetheart, you cold there? I'll warm you up." Foetid breath beneath a rough growl assailed me. I repressed the urge to turn away or vomit, knowing it would only provoke him further. Clammy warmth rubbed my side. My stomach clenched, fighting the numbness that spread through me until I was ice.

A beep sounded at my last keystroke. It was a welcome distraction from my self-analysis. As the thug moved away, I squinted at a screen I'd never seen before.

"It's asking for a password." My voice was husky from lack of use, or maybe it was from screaming silently inside.

"What? No, ...Oi! Nerd! You never said nothin' 'bout no flamin' password!"

Black wire glasses appeared above the divider between the teller cubes. A tuft of dark hair wobbled above a brow furrowed in concentration.

"Seriously, already? Hang on, how far has she got?" Glasses grimaced at me theatrically from his seat at the opposite counter, rolling eyes in the direction of the stale-breathed thug. I returned the sentiment, if only mentally. There was no way I wanted any of these aggressors believing I sympathised with them.

"I'm as far as the login for the manager's screen," I snapped, short breaths puffing through a clenched chest.

Get it over, quick and easy; then they'll be gone.

It was the mantra that had been running through my head for the past twenty minutes.

Get it over, over.

Behind the partition, another patron was being turned into a banana.

We thought we'd been well prepared for an armed robbery. The thin booklet on personal safety was required reading. Give them what they want, and they will leave. Sound the silent alarm behind your terminal.

Karen had tried to do that.

I refused to look at her desk again, my stomach heaving. HR's strategy hadn't worked this time. Maybe I should send them a memo on it, come Monday.

If I was still breathing then.

"Only the login? That's disappointing." Glasses' brow furrowed deeply. "She should have passed that, already. I gave you the codes for those, before...well," he waved a hand behind himself, where a body lay: Karen — the teller who had manned the desk where Glasses now sat before she was yanked from the line of hostages. A swell of emotion blurred my eyes. I blinked tears away angrily.

Don't think, don't think. Over. Get it over and done.

Focus.

Tapped the keyboard, wiggled the mouse. Breathe.

Don't engage. Don't.

"Passwords?"

I was proud my voice didn't shake. My logical brain informed me it was shock and nothing that was under my control. The emotional part didn't answer; it was as numb as the rest of me.

Glasses raised his eyebrows.

"Yes, ma'am."

He flicked a brief salute. A scrap of paper fluttered from his fingers, landing beside the keyboard.

"*Fluffy22*? Really?" I couldn't help commenting. "Cat or dog?"

"Likely the goldfish. Some people have no idea, truly," Glasses responded with a roll of his eyes. We shared a look. I realised what I was doing and quickly returned to the screen: Staring, willing tunnel vision.

Don't, don't.

Heavy footsteps reverberated behind me where the bank manager's office sat. A heavy hand clapped down on my shoulder. Too hot, too overly familiar. His thumb rubbed the sensitive spot on my collarbone, forcing an unwelcome shiver through me.

I willed myself still, to not react, desperate to return to the blank nothing that had consumed me only a moment before, though the urge to jerk away lingered when he spoke.

Deep and cold. The same voice I had heard beside Karen.

Before.

"How're we going, we in yet?"

"Not yet, boss; gotta put these in," Glasses indicated the passwords, "Then we should have full access."

I still couldn't believe it. These guys were going to bungle their own robbery. My screen had no way to access the electronic locks for the safe, and anyway, it was such a small branch. Surely, nothing they held would be sufficient to risk years of incarceration. Reflex had my mouth open to say as much until my brain kicked into gear. My mouth closed with a snap. The three men turned to look at me, and I started guiltily.

"Something you'd like to add, lass?" The question was delivered with some small humour and a touch of annoyance. I shook my head mutely.

"Right, let's get this show on the road."

I chanced a glimpse up at the man behind the robbery: tanned skin, longer-than-average dark hair, hard jaw. Tall and lean. You were supposed to remember details like that for the police, right? His face swivelled my way, displaying ice-cold eyes, unsuited to the rest of his handsome frame.

The devil within, I thought numbly. That wasn't a face that would be easy to forget. I'd have no trouble describing him later, I knew. With hands beginning to tremor from the proximity of the man responsible for the death of my friend, I entered the passwords as the prompts came up. A tiny box popped up in the centre of the screen that I had never seen before.

"...And we're in." Glasses leaned over the divider, meerkat style. "Thanks, love." He winked at me, tapping furiously on a portable keyboard he'd rolled out on the desktop. "Ta-daa."

With a dramatic flourish over his head and the tap of a final keystroke, my screen winked, flickered to blue, and reopened. The little cursor moved around with a mind of its own, opening areas, changing settings. Glasses was manipulating my computer remotely.

More tapping, a little head bobbing, and a clunk came from the rear of the office space — *the safe*. The lights flickered briefly, and I looked around. The three men moved away in a synchronised motion that made me wonder if they'd practised it. Suddenly left alone and grateful for it, I exhaled a long breath that left me more empty than before. One of the men sauntered back out, standing beside the last person in the row of hostages.

Every one of them tensed, and I wondered if they were thinking of the same sound as I did as it ricocheted around my head. Clangs and swearing came from the rear of the bank. I realised I knew less about the bank I'd worked in for three years than I had thought.

Distracted by a swirl of glitter, I looked over at the rows of patrons lining the wall opposite my station: the little girl tracing invisible pictures on the neutral carpet with a sparkling princess wand; a lone, glossy, red shoe, involuntarily discarded upon impact. A stockinged foot, partly visible, protruding behind a cubicle. I dragged my gaze away.

Sit still. Don't think. Don't.

A shadow flitted across the windows that looked out onto the street from the front of the small bank. From their positions on the floor pressed against the wall opposite the teller stations, customers — hostages — shifted uncomfortably, attempting to appear insignificant. Up top, I was exposed, the downlights above me driving sweat around my collar, though it ran down my back cold. I wasn't sure if it was fuelled by fear or heat.

My water bottle cooled my palms, and I slugged down water like a thirsty camel, placing it back on the desk. I shuffled pencils in their holder, ordering them neatly by height. It gave my hands something to do. I took a long, deep breath and tried to settle, to be calm. Letting my eyes close out the rest of the office, I focused on my breath, trying to ignore the sounds behind me. It took a few tries, but I almost had it down, the panic beginning to recede, until I remembered that Karen was the one who had taught me the technique.

My heart pounded anew as I tried to erase the image. Numb fingers fumbled my water bottle, slipping on the condensation coating the clear plastic. It spun in the air, too fast for water to escape, though its movement seemed slow enough to me.

I almost had one hand — who was I kidding; it was the tip of my finger — on the bottle when a loud clang startled me. I fumbled the bottle a second time, wide-eyed as it hit the floor, emptying its contents. I jerked as a small, black wooden box appeared in the corner of my vision and slid forward.

Tanned hands attached to thick forearms reached across my desk. I would have loved them if I hadn't known who they belonged to. I was a sucker for well-muscled forearms, but not at this moment. Fine, white linen sleeves, rolled to the elbows, looked so out of place — an involuntary glance once again gave the impression of a wealthy businessman, not a bank robber.

Murderer.

Gaze fixed, he cradled the box, caressed the lid. It was such an intimate gesture; it felt as though I was intruding on a personal moment. I inched away discreetly until the edge of my chair bit into the backs of my thighs.

Fear permeated the thickened air — from me, and the gallery on the floor. The man behind the robbery stared at the dark, little box with greedy eyes. Glasses appeared, hovering in my peripheral vision.

He annoyed me, and I wanted to bat him away. A twitch in the robber's shoulder left me thinking he felt the same.

Stop sympathising with them.

Reluctantly, one tanned hand released its prize, extended in a beseeching gesture. A tiny tremor quaked through the limb. With no small amount of ceremony, Glasses produced a minuscule key, placing it into the hollow cup of his upturned palm.

The little, silver scrap glinted dully — antique-looking — until the tip. I squinted and leaned forward, trying to discern the markings at the bottom of the filigree blade. The end curled upward, screwlike. The inserted key would have to be twisted or wound, like an old music box.

Reverently, the key was lowered to the lock, almost touching. Silence reigned; within the little cluster, no breath escaped.

The moment shattered abruptly, along with the glass of the large, street-front window. A dark shadow blasted through, into the foyer of the bank, showering everyone in glittering shards. Scarlet and indigo lights reflected in the glass littering the carpet. Voices cried out — a high, thin shriek piercing above the rest.

"Daddy!" A little sob accompanied the cry. The group surrounding me broke up, the small, black box forgotten in a surge of movement. The two men who had held the hostages at bay accompanied their leader toward the mess of glass, weapons fluidly drawn as one.

These men have worked together before.

I studied the changed scene before me as though I were the one behind glass; a shiny, black Jeep protruded into the cavity that used to be the front of the bank. Blue and red lights hung slightly lopsided, the odd flash blinding and disappearing in a staccato motion, adding to the surreality of the image.

Lots of extra attachments I was sure wouldn't be on a regular, stock model hung from the vehicle. A loud whoop came from within the open-topped cab, the flashing lights turned off, and everyone in the bank froze.

Two heads emerged from behind the black utility dash. One, a shag of blonde hair bearing a cheeky grin out of place in the sombre atmosphere. The other, a weather-worn face, covered in a beard that looked more suited to a motorcycle gang. He bore a resigned expression.

The shaggy-haired driver hoisted himself onto his seat in full view of the three men, who aimed their guns at him. His mouth moved, some throwaway line I missed. *What a cowboy.* The thieves evidently agreed; from my view of their backs as they moved forward, their leader shook his head, his fine shirt barely creasing with effort as he raised his weapon.

"Hold on there, John Wayne," he drawled with a tinge of sarcasm, "this here's my bank."

Shaggy gave a cocky, lopsided grin. "I've always fancied myself more as Wyatt Earp. At least he could shoot."

He held out a hand — rather pompously, I thought — and the man still seated in the passenger seat of the Jeep tossed him a long firearm. No expert on guns, I watched the exchange with fascination.

"Oh, let him have his small moment of glory."

Shaggy drew and aimed, managing to pose at the same time. I fought the urge to roll my eyes, unable to feel the fear I knew I should — entranced by the drama unfolding before me. Shaggy's firearm was matte black, matching the Jeep. Clean and pristine.

"And I half expected it to be a six-shooter." The dark man tilted his head briefly to the side. "Step aside, now. Your time in the limelight is over." A sideways glance to his team, speaking just loud enough that I could hear him, "It's time to go."

"Hold it, gents!" Shaggy seemed surprised he had lost control over the situation — if he'd ever had it. His partner started to stand also, groping the bench seat behind him when a sharp report broke the unreality of their playacting. The hostages ducked in a wave as the man to the left of the posse's leader fired a single shot.

Shaggy's partner disappeared beneath the dash. The young cop attempted to do the same, but seemed to slip, teetering comically sideways for a moment before toppling over the back of the driver's seat with a short yell. There was a thump as he landed. The moment the cop was down, the three men in front lowered their weapons, advancing towards the newly-created exit in unison.

Glasses scurried up, collected the key with a quick wink, and followed the team outside, flanked by the man with bad breath. A white transit van drew up to the curb, and the men disappeared inside.

The van moved off. I sat, frozen completely, unable to process the situation. Sirens approached from the opposite direction. Lights lit up the bank interior like Christmas, reflecting off broken glass scattered on the floor in a kaleidoscope of colour.

Reversing, the Jeep disappeared back through the hole it had created in the bank's only window, following the direction the white van had taken. Emergency vehicles rushed past in a string of flashing lights.

It's like something out of a movie.

Dazed hostages paused, watching. Glances were exchanged, though no one spoke. Fear and uncertainty still hung in the air. After a moment, the spell was broken, and movement resumed. Customers stirred, no longer cowering beneath armed aggressors. Soft chatter filled the ruined bank.

I knew I should ask them to sit alone, quietly, so their stories wouldn't be confused by each other's interpretations of what they had just endured. My training kicked in, my brain screaming at me to move, but I couldn't.

Glass tinkled as it was brushed from clothing. Swivelling slightly, I made to stand. On the desk behind me, stood the wooden box. Wouldn't the thieves be furious when they realised Glasses had taken the key but forgotten the box? One of the patrons who had been cowering against my counter leaned over to me.

"Looks like they left something important behind," he said with a sad smile. I nodded, still staring at the box, lost in thought. A tiny sob broke the murmur from the hostages, and we both looked up.

The little girl stood in the centre of the wreckage, her glitter wand drooping to brush the faded carpet, covered with a different sort of sparkle.

Eyes wide, I turned to the man who had spoken, recognising him as the owner of a local grocery store.

"I think they left behind more than one thing."

Silence fell, heavy as a shroud. Heads turned to the little girl who wandered aimlessly in the centre of the deconstructed bank, tears coursing down a face partially covered by dirty-blonde locks. Dust motes danced around the small figure in the afternoon light as brightly decorated police cars drew up along the bank front. Men swarmed toward the window.

The wand dropped to the floor.

"Daddy?"

READ CAL AND MILA'S STORY HERE:
www.books2read.com/Collision-LQP

POLITICS AND PAPERWORK

A BLUE BLOODED BROTHERS NOVELLA

Liam is constantly swamped beneath the politics of managing an elite task force. Now, given more downtime than he can handle, the ex-special ops sniper flounders to find purpose outside the strict rigours of his working day.

Selena has been Liam's best friend for nearly fifteen years. Elegant and intelligent, and a partner in her own law firm, she's helped Liam through difficult cases, as well as the aftermath of PTSD. Watching Liam drown in day-to-day life, Selena ups the stakes with a little flirting to restore life to the man she adores.

When a series of vandalisms target Selena, Liam is determined to keep the captivating solicitor safe, so long as she lets him. Intent on playing her game by his own rules, Liam risks an uncertain future for the woman he's always loved.

LIAM AND SELENA'S STORY WILL
CONTINUE IN RECKONING.

www.books2read.com/politicsandpaperwork

416

BLINDSIDED

As the youngest member of an elite task force team and built as big as they come, Danny is often underestimated. It's an image he encourages, despite sporting a genius level IQ. Currently screwing his boss' ex and with a big problem for authority, Danny is sent to professional development coaching. He hates the idea – he's got determination in spades to do what it takes in his job and personal life, and thrashes against it until he meets Laura, the sexy motivator who shows him he is worth more than what he believes. When the team begins working Operation Predator, Danny's moment of peace is shot to hell.

Danny is sent to professional coaching as part of his boss, Cal's, efforts to hold the team together after their last operation. When he discovers his motivator is the gorgeous jogger he's been working out with, Danny is determined to flirt his way through his coaching, stubbornly refusing to delve into personal truths he's been hiding from himself for years. He's relieved when he's placed on an undercover assignment – his preferred area of expertise.

Moving in with a group of gym junkies isn't a bad way to spend assignment – especially when he gets to hack as well. The group remove small change from banks, but Danny feels there is something bigger in the works – until he is spotted by Laura, who almost blows his cover. Pulled from his assignment, Danny is furious. Tensions rise during their coaching sessions as more odd hacks catch Danny's attention.

Their budding relationship is blown to pieces when he opts to go back undercover, determined not to let Laura distract him.

www.books2read.com/Blindsided-BBB2

TRICKSTER'S LAW

A child isn't born evil...is he?

Mischiefmaker, silver tongue, trickster... Mayhem follows Loki throughout the nine realms, earning him a reputation as a bringer of chaos. But there is more to Loki than mortals see, and life is boring for an immortal when no one really *gets him.*

A little mischief is harmless in the hands of a god, right?

Companion to Odin and Thor but shunned by the Norse gods of the Æsir, Loki still seeks their acceptance. No matter how many times he saves their supreme backsides, his every effort ends with a death threat casually tossed in his direction.

Increasing his attempts to impress the Æsir, Loki tires of their constant disdain despite his successes in their impossible challenges. So, he turns to what he does best: chaos.

Follow the trickster god Loki through the perfectly normal life of a disillusioned god, and find out what makes him NOT SO...EVIL.

THIS IS A STAND-ALONE NOVEL IN A COLLABORATION OF ORIGIN STORIES.
www.books2read.com/TrickstersLaw